To Sophie

Wrangling the Cowboy's Heart

Enjoy!
Leah Vale
x

WRANGLING THE COWBOY'S HEART

A RODEO ROMEOS ROMANCE

LEAH VALE

Wrangling the Cowboy's Heart
Copyright© 2020 Leah Vale
Tule Publishing First Printing, June 2020

The Tule Publishing, Inc.

ALL RIGHTS RESERVED

First Publication by Tule Publishing 2020

Cover design by Lee Hyat Designs

No part of this book may be used or reproduced in any manner whatsoever without written permission except in the case of brief quotations embodied in critical articles and reviews.

This is a work of fiction. Names, characters, places, and incidents are products of the author's imagination or are used fictitiously. Any resemblance to actual events, locales, organizations, or persons, living or dead, is entirely coincidental.

ISBN: 978-1-951786-80-9

CHAPTER ONE

"Someone get a rope on him, the chute gate isn't latched," Liam Neisson shouted as he clamored over the bucking chute where bulls and broncs burst into the Pineville, Oregon, rodeo arena. He'd just sent his newest, and rowdiest, bucking horse into the chute.

And Wild Bill wasn't having it.

Rebelling against the confines of the metal-railed bucking chute, the big, brown-and-white pinto gelding tossed his head repeatedly, preventing Liam's brother Drew from getting his lasso over the horse's head. Wild Bill took exception to the attempts, rolling his eyes and blowing out puffs of agitated breaths that misted in the crisp September morning air. Clearly, Wild Bill had decided to live up to his name. But Liam needed to acclimate the bronc to the chutes and noise of the arena before the start of the High Desert Rodeo in two days.

Liam balanced himself on the gate rails on the arena side of the chute and reached for the spring-loaded lever latch. Before he could secure the latch, Wild Bill threw his shoulder into the gate and sent it swinging open. It was all Liam could do to retain his grip and ride the gate backward as the gelding burst into the arena in a bucking frenzy. Even without a sheepskin flank strap fastened behind the widest part of the horse's abdomen, let alone a rider on his back, the bronc kicked wild and high.

Liam grinned. The way the horse clearly loved to buck was exactly why he had blown a huge chunk of the budget his grandfather had allocated him for this season's broncos on Wild Bill at auction. Now all Liam had to do was find a stud who could buck as well as Wild Bill for his breeding program. Then he would be able to prove to his grandfather once and for all that the Wright Ranch could be known for supplying the rankest bucking horses as well as standout bucking bulls.

His older brother Ian might be the perfect Neisson to inherit the job of running the entire Wright Ranch rodeo rough stock operation, but Liam was determined to bring value to the ranch, also, with his broncs.

It was the least he could do after failing to save his mother from being injured by one of his grandfather's bulls. Injuries that had ultimately proved fatal.

As much as Liam would have liked to watch Wild Bill buck until he wore himself out, the start of the High Desert County regional rodeo was only two days away, so the arena was downright crowded. The rodeo court had been practicing one of their mounted flag-bearing routines and had to scatter to avoid the bronc's unpredictable path. A roping team who'd been practicing their throws were caught with their ropes on the dirt and had no choice but to head to the rails as they rushed to recoil their lassos.

"Liam! Here!" Drew held out the lasso he'd recoiled from his spot on the catwalk.

Liam reached across the empty chute the gate had come to rest against and grabbed the lasso from his younger brother. He jumped down from the gate onto the deep loam of the arena and extracted himself from between the gate and chute railing.

Before he could start out into the arena after Bill, a blur of buckskin and long dark brunette hair blasted past him, pelting him with small clods of dirt.

Amanda Rodrigues. His little sister's best friend for as long as he could remember rode her barrel racer quarter horse, Rumbles, at a full gallop toward Wild Bill. Her pale pink western-style shirt billowed and the late morning sun sparked off her bedazzled jeans pockets as she leaned forward in the saddle. Her cream felt cowboy hat flew from her head, fully unleashing her hair in a dark flag streaming gloriously behind her.

"Amanda, don't!" Liam shouted. In the short time he'd had the gelding, Liam had learned Wild Bill was long on attitude and short on manners.

As if putting Liam's thoughts to action, Wild Bill twisted in midair to aim his rear hooves toward Amanda and Rumbles. The nimble barrel horse cut sideways, deftly avoiding Bill's flying hooves but nearly unseated Amanda.

His heart in his throat, Liam ran toward them as fast as the soft footing allowed and started swinging the lasso loop over his head. But he was still too far away to make an effective throw.

Liam's gut twisted. He couldn't allow anyone to get hurt, especially his sister's headstrong best friend.

Despite his warning and the gelding's erratic leaps and bucks, Amanda guided her smaller mare next to the bronc and leaned sideways in the saddle, reaching for his halter. The woman had no sense.

"No, Amanda!" Liam yelled, willing her to listen to him.

If she actually got a hold of the halter, one swing of Wild Bill's head would yank her clean out of the saddle and probably dislocate her arm. Bill had draft horse somewhere in his lineage, evident in his size and strength. His temperament was one hundred percent ornery-ass horse.

Before Liam could get close enough to throw his lasso, Amanda made another grab for Wild Bill's halter. Liam's pulse stuttered. It figured she hadn't listened to him. While growing up, Amanda and Caitlin only ever listened to Ian. And Grandfather, of course.

Swinging the lasso faster to compensate for the distance his throw would have to cover, Liam realized Amanda wasn't actually trying to grab Wild Bill's halter, she was trying to clip a lead line onto the bronc.

Anchored by a hand gripping her saddle horn, she leaned what seemed impossibly far to the side and timed her attempts to Bill's head tosses as he bucked. The metallic click of the lead line fastener successfully finding purchase on one of the halter's O-rings reached him and Amanda righted herself in the saddle. With lightning-fast movements she wrapped the other end of the lead around her saddle horn.

Okay, maybe she had a *little* sense.

She urged Rumbles into an easy canter, and the mare's forward momentum forced Wild Bill to settle and follow along at the end of the lead line.

Liam let the lasso fall slack at his side as Amanda eased Rumbles and Wild Bill down to a trot, then a walk. She slowly shortened the lead rope until the big gelding's nose was at her knee and she reined her mare in an easy turn, heading back toward where he stood.

"Woot! Amanda, you rock," Drew said as he ran up beside Liam. He'd retrieved Amanda's hat from the dirt and was waving it above his head.

The others in the arena whooped and clapped.

Liam's gaze returned to Amanda and stuck. He should be watching his gelding's gait for any sign of injury that might have been sustained while breaking out of the chute, but Liam couldn't drag his attention from the beautiful woman riding her buckskin toward him.

No longer restrained by the cowboy hat she'd lost, her long, dark brunette curls bounced in a wild cloud around her heart-shaped face. She was positively beaming with blatant satisfaction for successfully wrangling his wayward bronc.

Damn, when the hell had she become so pretty?

Actually, he knew exactly when. Earlier that summer at the Pineville Rodeo, Liam had been knocked back on his boot heels by the realization that the little dark-haired girl who'd practically lived at the Wright Ranch aiding and abetting his sister in her shenanigans had grown into a real beauty. Beautiful and fearless.

The memory of Amanda's hand pressed against his chest,

right over his heart, had haunted him since the day she'd helped Caitlin stop him from giving Bodie Hadley what he deserved. At least what Liam had thought Bodie deserved at the time. But now that it was clear how much Caitlin loved Bodie, and because Liam loved his sister, Bodie was officially off the hook for his part in cousin Charlie's death. Liam had immediately squashed the zing of attraction Amanda's touch had sent through him at the time because she was *Amanda*.

"You're catchin' flies, bro."

Snapping his mouth shut, Liam yanked his attention from Amanda and leveled his best glare at Drew for using one of their youngest brother Alec's favorite jabs. The anger always lurking just below Liam's skin flared, itchy and hot. It was as though an invisible, full-body rash had engulfed him the day he'd simply stood frozen in place and watched his grandfather's best bucking bull chase his mom and sister down in the paddock Liam had been repairing. Mom had saved Caitlin with a shove, but no one had been near enough to save Mom. No one except him, and he had just stood there and watched.

From that day forward, Liam had been angry. Angry at himself for not leaping to action the second the bull had entered the paddock on the heels of his mom and sister. Angry at the strangling powerlessness that had consumed him in that moment and that he'd never managed to shake. Angry that he secretly believed he'd lost his chance to do what he wanted in life, whatever that might have been, when he'd failed to act quickly enough to save his mom from harm. He needed to stay on the ranch to ensure everyone else he cared about stayed safe.

Drew held up his empty hand as if in surrender and took a step back. "Easy. Nothing wrong with admiring a pretty lady."

Liam curled his lip at his brother for reading him with so little effort.

Drew turned his attention to Amanda as she approached and said loudly enough for her to hear, "Pretty and badass!"

Amanda grinned and acknowledged the compliment with a flourishing bow over her saddle horn.

Brushing the arena dirt from her cowboy hat's felt, Drew stepped toward her. "You are my hero, Amanda Rodrigues." He handed her the hat.

She took her hat and returned it to her head, once again containing her wild curls. "You are easily impressed, Drew Neisson."

His grin said she wasn't wrong.

Liam rolled his eyes at his clown of a brother and set to recoiling the lasso he hadn't had the chance to use with quick, jerky movements.

Amanda lifted the reins and urged Rumbles and Wild Bill forward. Stopping in front of Liam, she unwound the lead rope she'd attached to the gelding's halter from her saddle horn and handed it to him. "This big guy belongs to you, I believe."

He glared at the braided, red nylon lead in her hand for a long moment before handing the lasso to Drew and taking the lead from her. He should have been quicker throwing the chute gate latch home. He should have had a rope on Wild

Bill before sending him into the chute. He should have been the one to wrangle the gelding to keep those in the arena safe.

His entire life was one big *should have.*

Amanda made a noise in the back of her throat. "You're welcome."

He met her gaze. "You could have been hurt." When had her eyes turned such a beautiful, rich shade of chocolate brown?

She smiled widely and made an all-encompassing gesture at the arena. "Rodeo."

He had to work at holding on to his irritation. She was right, yet again. By definition, rodeos were dangerous in some shape or form. But it was up to people like him to make the arena as safe as possible. His rough stock was his responsibility.

And he should have known Amanda wouldn't listen to him when he'd yelled for her to stop. She had always been too stubborn and willful for her own good. She and Caitlin had been a real handful.

"Why are you here?" His gaze traveled over her pink western-style shirt and jeans, doing his best to ignore the very feminine shape beneath them. "You aren't a member of this rodeo's court."

Her grin said she was tickled he'd noticed. How could he not when she looked so delectable in fringes and sequins?

"Nope. Not this rodeo. Rumbles and I were practicing our starts." She patted her buckskin mare's sleek neck and smoothed her black mane. "Rumbles is rusty with me spending so much time working with Whiskey Throttle."

Liam's focus was instantly on what Amanda was saying rather than on how her mouth looked as she said it. Amanda's uncle, Federico "Old Red" Rodrigues, had just that morning been complaining to Liam about how the new stud he had acquired for their barrel horse breeding program would rather buck than run barrels.

The exact kind of stallion Liam needed for his bronc breeding program.

Now he just needed to convince Amanda to sell the horse to him. Red had told him that, as of her twenty-fifth birthday, Amanda was the boss at the Sky High Ranch per her late parents' will. And Amanda was not only known for being very attached to her horses, but also for refusing to give up on any of them. Or anything, for that matter.

Taking a beat to make sure the excitement building inside him didn't leak into his voice, Liam smoothed a hand over Wild Bill's satiny muzzle. The gelding had calmed considerably since bursting from the bucking chute but he was still blowing hard from his exertion.

"Whiskey Throttle?" he asked as casually as he could.

"My new stallion. He's sweet as pie, but…" She trailed off, fiddling with her reins as if loath to admit the horse's failings.

Being a bucking machine was no failing in Liam's book, it was money in the bank. "But?" he prompted.

She heaved a sigh. "He's a little rough around the edges."

"How so?" he pressed. He wanted to hear her say the words.

"He's not entirely trained to the saddle."

That was one way to say the horse tried to launch anyone to the moon who dared to climb on his back. Liam nodded, all sage-like. But inside, anticipation bubbled.

Drew slung the now coiled lasso over his shoulder. "Is he the big red roan who keeps putting you in the dirt? Old Red says there's no way in hell you'll break that one of bucking."

Liam shot his brother a glare. Amanda would never agree to sell the horse if she believed she'd failed somehow.

"I don't *break* my horses, Drew. I *train* them." She shifted in the saddle and stroked Rumbles's mane again. "I just need more time with him."

Drew gestured up at her left wrist. "You sure you'll survive him?"

Liam noticed the athletic tape her wrist was wrapped in peeking from beneath the cuff of her sleeve. She'd been hurt. His insides twisted again, just like they had when she'd reached for Wild Bill's halter. He didn't like the thought of Amanda hurt.

She glanced down at her tapped wrist. "Absolutely. This is nothing." But she tugged her cuff down and crossed her other wrist over it as if to hide the injury.

Drew scoffed, clearly not buying Amanda's bravado any more than Liam was. "Yeah, well, good luck with that." He hitched the lasso higher on his shoulder. "And good luck with your races this weekend."

"Thanks, Drew."

Drew tipped his black cowboy hat to her and sauntered away.

Liam scratched Bill's cheek beneath his halter and decided to test the waters. "You know, I just happen to be on the hunt for a new stud for my bucking horse program."

Amanda uncrossed her wrists and tugged at her cuff again. "So?"

"So..." Liam dropped his gaze to Wild Bill and freed a hank of the gelding's dark brown forelock from beneath the blue nylon halter. "If you decide you can't *train* the buck out of Whiskey Throttle, I'd consider buying him from you."

"You'd consider it?"

Her sharp tone brought his gaze back to hers to see if he'd offended her. He had. He mentally shrugged. He'd rather have her angry with him than injured by a horse meant more for the bucking bronc circuit than barrel racing or even just pleasure riding. "If he checks out, of course."

"Of course."

Yep, she was offended. "I can stop by your place sometime and take a look at him—"

"No need, Liam. I'll have Whiskey running barrels by the end of the month."

The woman did like a challenge. Liam grinned up at her. "I look forward to seeing that. And if not, I'll buy him from you."

"If he checks out." Her tone dripped sarcasm.

"Of course." He mimicked her, minus the sarcasm, his grin widening.

The horse was as good as his, if what Red said about the stallion refusing to be ridden was true. Which Liam didn't doubt, because if anyone around here knew their horseflesh, it was Old Red.

The only problem Liam could foresee was Amanda's stubbornness and refusal to admit defeat. Not to mention his admiration for her. This was Amanda, after all.

Gathering her irritation along with Rumbles's reins, Amanda wheeled Rumbles away from the big dumb animal. And she was not referring to the big brown-and-white gelding.

Of all of her best friend Caitlin's brothers, Liam had always drawn her eye. Six foot one of ranch-honed muscle, he had the standard issue Neisson blond-haired, blue-eyed good looks. But ever since his grandfather's prized bucking bull trampled his mom right in front of him, he'd carried his anger around like a split-rail fence post on his shoulders for all to see.

It hurt her heart.

But his doubting her abilities stirred something completely opposite within her. There was no way she'd simply hand over her beautiful roan stallion to him. Not that he wouldn't pay her a fair price or treat Whiskey Throttle well. She knew without a doubt he loved horses as much as she did. The way he'd calmed the big gelding after she'd returned it to him showed her as much.

But she wouldn't sell him the stallion Uncle Red had used all their cash reserves to purchase for her. She'd prove to Liam that not only could she train the stallion to saddle, she'd turn him into a champion barrel racer whose progeny would sell for top dollar.

The dull throb in her wrist, injured when Whiskey had bucked her off the last time she'd tried to ride him, called her delusional. She ignored it. She was a master at ignoring any and all pain. She'd had lots of practice since the day her parents' small plane had crashed and taken them from her when she was a whopping six years old. Though every now and again the dull throb that had settled in her chest when her parents hadn't come home forced its way into her consciousness.

Spotting Uncle Red standing near the arena's center entrance, gesturing for her to come to him, Amanda set Rumbles to an easy canter toward him. As soon as she reached him Red waved a folded piece of paper at her.

"What is that?"

Red held the paper up to her. "Something you need to read. Now."

Amanda took the paper. "Did you see us run down Liam's new bronc? Rumbles dodged that big gelding's kicks all by himself."

"I saw. You did good, darlin'. You did your parents proud. But you need to read that, Amanda." Red pointed at what she now saw was an official-looking letter on thick, stiff paper.

Always warmed by the praise of the man who'd raised her from the age of six, Amanda unfolded the letter and read it.

Her heart stalled and her breath froze in her lungs.

The letter was from a lawyer in Portland, informing her that his client, who wished to remain anonymous, held a due-on-demand promissory note on her ranch. And he was calling it in. Her parents must have borrowed money from this person, when they were buying the ranch.

Dread, icy cold and sickening, spread through her until her fingertips tingled. She didn't have the money he was demanding. Not even close. They'd spent almost everything they had on Whiskey Throttle. Red had told her at the time they needed to spend money to make money.

She met her uncle's gaze. "Do you know who this anonymous note holder is?"

Red ran a gnarled, life-worn hand over his face, knocking his gray cowboy hat askew. "No, I don't. I wasn't around here much then because I was rodeoing full time. All I knew at the time was that your folks had found a ranch they'd fallen in love with, but didn't have the capital for. Then they did. I'd always assumed they'd secured a loan directly from the bank. Because that's where the payments pulled directly from the trust they'd set up went to."

Amanda reread the letter, but other than the lawyer's name and the name of his firm, there was definitely no hint to the person's identity. "Do you have any idea at all who it could be?"

Uncle Red heaved a sigh and straightened his hat. "My guess would be the loan came from a friend of your father's. Your dad got to know all sorts of people when he was getting his pilot's license. He was asking pretty much everyone he knew for help to buy the ranch and get it up and running. I was living hand to horse's mouth then and couldn't help, and our parents—as well as your mom's folks—hadn't left anything behind other than what they'd taught us about hard work."

The dread settled heavily in the pit of her stomach. No way could she simply turn over her home to a complete stranger.

She dismounted and considered the letter again. "I guess we could go to the bank and see if we could get a loan from them to pay this person off."

Red shook his head. "I wouldn't get your hopes up about being able to mortgage property that already has a promissory note attached to it. But it wouldn't hurt to try, though, I suppose. Only you'll have to do it by your lonesome. I have to leave today to head up to the Calgary rodeo I'm working as an event judge at, remember?"

She nodded, but she had forgotten. Red had been leaving a lot, lately. The sinking feeling in her stomach intensified. She rattled the paper. "But why call in the note now? Why not after Mom and Dad's plane crash?"

Red shook his head and stared off into the arena. "I don't know. But that land sure is valuable. Especially buttin' up against the Wright Ranch on one side and a vast tract owned by the Bureau of Land Management on the other."

Red's mention of Caitlin's home gave Amanda an idea. There was only one person she could think of who could help her.

But he never did anything without getting something in return.

CHAPTER TWO

THE NEXT MORNING Amanda was two steps into the mudroom attached to the kitchen of the Wright Ranch's massive main house before it occurred to her she should have used the front door.

And knocked.

And driven her truck instead of her ATV so her hair wouldn't be a wild mess.

She looked down at herself. She also had mud splatters all over her jeans. But having spent nearly the entirety of her youth popping in and out of the huge house to see Caitlin, the use of propriety today hadn't even occurred to her.

She wasn't here to see her best friend, however, and she needed to go about this visit the right way. With the start of the High Desert Rodeo tomorrow, she didn't have time to put this off long enough to go back home and clean up, but the least she could do was go around to the front door.

She turned on her heel to go back out the way she'd come in, intent on making the hike around the ten-thousand-plus-foot main house to the front door when a deep voice stopped her.

"Caitlin's not here, Amanda."

Ian. The oldest of the Neisson siblings. She'd been dreading possibly running into Liam, the next oldest Neisson sibling. She was embarrassed enough having a barrel racer stud she couldn't ride. Having to admit to him she needed help with the note on her ranch that was being called in would be too much. She blew out the breath she'd unconsciously been holding and turned again toward the kitchen.

Smoothing her hair down as she rounded the stone wall that separated the mudroom from the gourmet kitchen, she spotted Ian seated at the kitchen bar on one of four upholstered stools. He had a cup of coffee, paperwork, and his dark brown cowboy hat spread on the black and brown flecked granite before him, a pen in his hand.

"Hey, Ian. I'm sorry to disturb you. I should have knocked, or gone around front or—"

He stopped her with a wave of his hand. "Nonsense. You're always welcome. And I saw you pull up on your ATV." He hitched his head to the wall of windows in what they called the breakfast nook but was large enough for a rough-hewn table capable of seating ten. The actual dining room table, located deeper in the house, accommodated twice that. Thomas Wright liked his family close, and had built a house big enough for all of them.

Ian turned the papers directly in front of him on the counter face down. "Caitlin is over at the Hadley spread. With Bodie," he added unnecessarily.

Having spoken to Caitlin on the phone this morning before driving over, Amanda already knew Caitlin wasn't here. And who was. But she hadn't told Cait about the letter.

Amanda wanted to know her options first. And Caitlin had enough on her plate with her engagement party this upcoming weekend.

"Actually, I'm not here to see Caitlin." Amanda moved to stand at the rounded end of the bar, worrying her hands in front of her.

Ian's ever-perceptive dark blue gaze flicked down to her hands, lingering on her taped wrist, then back up.

He set his pen down. "Is there anything I can help you with?"

She smiled. He'd always extended his oldest brother protectiveness to her not just simply because she was his sister's friend, but because that was Ian. He took care of those around him.

For a split second she thought of showing him the lawyer's letter, of letting him help her keep her home, but he hadn't been his usual focused, unflappable self this summer and she didn't want to add to whatever was burdening him.

"Thanks, but no. I need to speak to your grandpa."

Ian's blond eyebrows shot toward his even blonder hair, creased and flattened by his cowboy hat. She understood his surprise. While Thomas Wright had never been anything but kind and welcoming toward her, she had never, in all the time she had been coming over here—which was pretty much her entire life—specifically sought out the wealthy patriarch of the Wright and Neisson clan. She had never needed to.

Until now.

"Is everything okay?" Ian asked.

Not at all. "Oh, yeah." The folded letter from the lawyer burned like a heated brand in her back pocket. "I just need to—um—talk to him."

Ian considered her long enough she started to fidget, but she kept her hand from the letter and her mouth shut to any more explanation.

Picking up his pen again, Ian said, "I'm not entirely sure where Grandfather is at this exact moment, but Liam was looking for him earlier, so he can probably tell you."

Amanda's breath hitched. Crud. So much for avoiding Liam. "Great. Okay, thanks, Ian."

"No problem."

He continued to watch her instead of going back to his paperwork, so Amanda hurried out of the big kitchen and headed down one of the two, long hallways that branched off in opposite directions from the main entrance foyer. She and Caitlin used to roller-skate down them, each starting at the end of one and colliding in the middle. The texture of the slate floor always made such a satisfying rumble beneath their wheels.

But today, the rap of her boot heels on the slate made her wince and pray she wasn't tracking mud through the beautiful house.

Her attention on her feet, she smacked right into a big, hard chest with enough force to make him *oomph*.

"Amanda?" Liam.

"Oh, geez, Liam. Sorry. But you're just the man I was looking for."

His hands came up and settled on her hips, then dropped

away just as quickly. "Really?"

Intensely aware of his size and heat, she took a step back. Then another. "Um, yes. Ian said you'd know where your grandfather is."

"I'm not his secretary."

Ian's or their grandfather's? She supposed it didn't matter. "Ian didn't say you were. Just that you'd been looking for him, also, earlier."

Liam made a noise that was part acknowledgement and a lot disparaging. "He's in his office."

"In the bull barn?"

"No, this one." Liam aimed a thumb at the room he'd suddenly emerged from.

"Thanks, Liam." She stepped around him but he caught her by the elbow.

Raising her arm with surprising gentleness, as if she were one of his horses with an injured leg, he nudged her sleeve cuff back from her taped wrist.

"How's the wrist?"

The tape was filthy and her cheeks heated. Why hadn't she thought more about her appearance before she left home? She mentally kicked herself for not putting on a clean wrap. Or better yet, taken it off completely. But she hadn't expected Liam to be here. He should be at the rodeo grounds with his horses.

He slid his palm beneath hers, straightening her fingers, probably checking for swelling. His obvious concern did funny things to her stomach. Things she didn't like because she couldn't control them.

She eased her arm from his grasp. "I'm fine. It's fine. It's nothing."

He made another noise in his throat, this one disbelieving. "There's no reason to own an animal that is going to hurt you, Amanda."

"Says a man who owns a dozen animals who are literally bred to dump people on their heads." She waved the notion off. "And Whiskey Throttle didn't hurt me. I hurt myself by falling off."

"Getting bucked off is a sight worse than falling off."

"Both end with me in the dirt, though, right?" Why did he make her sweat so? She eased away from him again.

His frown deepened. "I'll give you ten percent more than you paid for him."

"Shouldn't you ask what I paid, first?"

He scoffed and gave her a look that said he already knew exactly what she paid for the big red stallion.

Of course he did. He was Thomas Wright's grandson. Liam probably knew more about her new stud than she did.

If only worrying about her newest horse was the most pressing thing in her life. Even if Liam paid her double, it wouldn't be enough to pay back the note.

She pulled in a steadying breath. "As fun as it is to horse wrangle with you, as I said, I'm here to see your grandfather."

"Come in and see me then, Amanda," a very deep, very gruff voice called from within the room Liam had emerged from.

While she had known Thomas Wright her entire life to

be nothing but, well, grandfatherly, toward her, he always made her quake in her boots. Probably because she'd mostly only been called in front of him when she and Caitlin were in trouble. She glanced up at Liam and found him smiling at her knowingly.

She so rarely saw him smile that the sight rocked her back. The man was beautiful scowling. Smiling, he stole her breath.

"Need backup?"

Keeping her voice low, she replied tartly, "No, I do not need backup." But she did wish Caitlin were here with her.

Thomas doted on his lone granddaughter, even when they'd been up to no good.

"Suit yourself." Liam waved a hand toward the open door.

Squaring her shoulders, Amanda entered the large, dark wood-paneled office. Thomas was seated behind an oversized, ornately carved desk looking very much like the chairman of the board of a Fortune 500 corporation. A western Fortune 500 corporation, the point driven home by his crisp, white western-style long-sleeve shirt and black bolero tie with silver accents.

He set aside the paperwork in his hand. "How can I help you?"

"I'm sorry to bother you, Mr. Wright—"

He held up a hand and stopped her. "Please, Amanda, you are an adult, now, and a rancher in your own right. Call me Thomas."

Her throat constricted. It had only been a few weeks

since her twenty-fifth birthday when she'd become the official owner of the Sky High Ranch, and it hadn't completely sunk in. It was one thing for her uncle to acknowledge her as the sole owner, and something completely different for Thomas to do so. She simply nodded and pulled the letter from her back pocket.

Unfolding the crisp cream paper, she said, "I received this in the mail." She handed him the letter across the desk.

He took the paper and indicated she should take a seat in one of the dark leather upholstered, nail-embossed chairs facing the desk.

His sharp gaze traveled quickly over the page then jumped back to hers as she sat down. "Do you want to know if I am the note holder?"

She opened her mouth, but realized in all honesty she couldn't deny the suspicion.

He purposefully laid the letter on the desk in front of him. "How long have you known me, Amanda?"

"For as long as I can remember, sir." She put voice to her earlier thought.

"Have you ever known me to hide behind anyone, let alone a lawyer, in my business dealings?"

"No, sir."

He sat back against his big desk chair, making the well-stuffed leather creak. "Exactly."

Amanda nodded, but was niggled by the fact Thomas didn't flat-out deny that he was the note holder.

He gestured to the letter. "This anonymous note holder, whomever he might be, has very curious timing. Very curious."

She also thought it interesting Thomas would assume the promissory note holder to be a man, but kept her mouth shut.

"I'm also assuming, since you are here, you have no idea who he is."

She forcibly squashed her doubts about Thomas. "None, sir. And neither does Uncle Red. We searched yesterday before Red had to leave for Calgary, but couldn't find any mention of a partner amongst my parents' documents."

"I can certainly make some inquiries." He rocked in his chair a few times. "Do you have the capital to cover the note?"

"Not even close, sir."

He nodded as if she'd stated a universal fact. What rodeoing rancher had a surplus of cash? Actually, he did, but Thomas Wright and his family were notable exceptions.

He rested his elbows on the arms of his chair and tented his fingers in front of him. "Any thoughts as to what you will do if this note proves valid?"

"I know what I don't want to do. No way will I simply turn over my parents' ranch for a fraction of its worth to a complete stranger."

"Your ranch, Amanda. Sky High is your ranch now."

Tears burned behind her eyes. Her parents had wanted the ranch they'd built to be hers. But it was so much more. It was the only home she'd ever known. The only home she'd ever wanted.

Thomas sat forward, his steely gaze intent on hers.

"Would you consider selling your ranch to someone you know? Someone who would pay off the promissory note as part of the deal and allow you and Red to retain ownership of the livestock and continue living on the ranch, running it as ranch managers?"

Hope flared hot and bright inside her. "You would do that for us?" She didn't doubt for a moment he was the someone he'd referred to.

She'd known there would be a price to any help Thomas might offer, but being able to pay off the note, retaining ownership of her animals, and staying in her home was more than she'd hoped for.

"It makes sense, Amanda. Your land is quality. And butts up against mine. So, yes. Assuming the buildings and fencing are up to my standards." He leaned to the side and looked toward the open door behind her. "Liam?"

Amanda turned and looked over her shoulder as Liam almost instantly appeared in the doorway. Had he been lurking outside his grandfather's office, listening the whole time?

"Yes?"

"I'd like you to inspect the Sky High structures and fencing to see if they meet the Wright Ranch's standards."

"And if they don't?"

No questions about why Thomas would want such a thing. He had been listening.

"I'll leave the answer of that up to you."

Liam's gaze flicked to hers, his expression unreadable.

Amanda's heart sank. Of all the Neissons on this ranch,

Liam was the most impossible to please.

THE FLICKER OF sheer terror in Amanda's chocolate-brown eyes doused the fire of excitement that had ignited inside Liam when he'd overheard her predicament. All he could think was that she would definitely sell her new stud to him now. She would need money to ready the ranch for sale, be it to his grandfather or anyone else. But seeing her so distressed did weird things to his insides.

He shut the sensation down. This was Amanda, after all. His insides shouldn't be feeling anything toward the woman who'd practically grown up on the Wright Ranch with his sister. She was also one of the most capable people he knew. She could take care of herself.

His grandfather stood and said, "Do you mind if I make a copy of this letter, Amanda?"

"No, of course not," she answered with ease, but Liam couldn't help but notice how she worried her hands in her lap.

Grandfather went to the printer set up on the credenza built into the bookcase consuming the wall to his right. He made a copy of the letter, then held the original out to Amanda. Before she could rise from her chair, Liam stepped past her and took the letter. He wanted to know exactly what it said and he didn't trust Amanda to share it with him.

Grandfather gave him an approving nod. "Liam will see you out, Amanda."

She rose, her hands twining together again. "Thank you again, Mr.—Thomas."

"We'll talk again after Liam makes his assessment."

Liam glanced up from the letter he was quickly reading in time to catch the look of undeniable dread she shot him. *Too bad, sweetheart.* She was stuck with him, because the only person he wanted to impress here was his grandfather. It was the least he could do after failing his mom.

Liam gestured for Amanda to precede him out of the office. She snatched the letter from him on her way by. He had to suppress his grin. She still was a real fireplug.

He followed her down the hall and into the kitchen, his gaze inadvertently glued to her perfectly rounded backside accentuated by her Wranglers. Had anyone asked him earlier what Amanda Rodrigues's best asset was, he would have said her eye for horseflesh. And her hair. The woman had amazing hair, all long, shiny mahogany curls. Now, he had to admit her backside was her glory.

Huh. He was a butt guy.

"Liam, do you have a moment?"

Ian's voice yanked Liam out of his booty study. His oldest sibling was seated at the kitchen counter bar, stacks of paper and a cup of coffee in front of him.

Liam acknowledged him with a hitch of his chin. "Just. What do you need?"

Ian glanced meaningfully at Amanda, who had stopped also when Ian first spoke.

Liam touched her trim waist. He had to squelch the urge to caress her there.

She raised a dark brow at him.

"How did you come over?"

"ATV."

"Can you wait for me by the garage?"

Both brows went up.

Of course. They had more than one. "The toy garage."

"You're coming over with me now?"

"Better now than after the county rodeo starts."

She harrumphed by way of acknowledgement and started for the back door. "See you, Ian."

"Amanda."

Liam waited to hear the mudroom door open and close before he moved toward his brother. "What do you need?"

Ian turned a stack of papers face down before angling toward Liam. "Are you heading back to the rodeo grounds?"

"No. I'm supposed to inspect Sky High."

Ian tucked his chin.

"I know, right? Turns out Amanda's folks had a silent partner who held a promissory note and he's called it due."

"After Amanda took ownership."

"Exactly. Obviously, she doesn't have the cash, and rather than just roll over for whoever this jerk is, she asked Grandfather for help."

"In paying off the note?"

"In buying the ranch. She'd rather have someone she knows buy it than a stranger."

Ian rubbed at his scruff of a beard. "She's proud."

"Ya think?"

"Any idea who the note holder is?"

"Nope. Grandfather is going to look into it."

Ian nodded, clearly mulling things over. "Do me a favor, will you?"

"What?"

"Can you—on the sly—look for any sign of theft at Sky High?"

"Theft?"

"As in anything that has gone missing from the ranch. Specifically involving their barrel racer breeding program."

Liam eyed the papers Ian had turned face down. "What have you gotten yourself involved in, Ian?"

"I'll tell you later. Can you do it?"

"Of course. No problem."

"Thanks, Liam. I'll owe you."

His mind swirling with possibilities, Liam started for the door Amanda had left through.

"And Liam?" Ian stopped him.

"What?"

"Be good to Amanda. She deserves it."

Liam saluted his brother. Of course he'd be good to Amanda. She was their little sister's best friend. And the owner of the horse he meant to get his hands on.

CHAPTER THREE

THE WARMTH OF the early September sun had nothing to do with the sweat making Amanda's palms damp on the ATV's handlebar grips. And she didn't need the roar of Liam's four-wheeler to be aware of his presence behind her. She'd never before worried about the appearance of her ranch. Even growing up next to the showcase that was the Wright Ranch, she'd always been proud of her and Red's spread. Her parents had built a comfortable, functional ranch that produced the highest quality barrel racers. What could matter more?

What Thomas Wright thought of it, that was what. Or, more immediately, what Liam thought of it.

She glanced over her shoulder at the man driving the ATV behind her. What she could see of his handsome face was impassive. He'd donned a black cowboy hat and mirrored sunglasses for the fairly short trip across rolling pasture land to her ranch. At least, what was her ranch for now. Her throat constricted and her lungs burned with the impending loss. This was the only home she'd ever known.

If Liam, and ultimately his grandfather, didn't approve of her place, then what? She and Red would have no choice but to sell everything they could and turn the entire ranch over to the note holder.

Liam would get Whiskey Throttle then for sure. There was no way he would let anyone else buy a horse that had caught his eye.

Fighting the sickening twist of helplessness building in her stomach, Amanda turned her attention back to the slight rise she'd steered her ATV toward and the split-rail fence atop it that separated Sky High and the Wright Ranch. The irrigated ryegrass, yellowed by the sun and the season, crumbled easily beneath the ATV's wheels. She adjusted her course and steered toward the gate Thomas and her parents had installed in the fence when it had become clear she and Caitlin were going to be more than just school bus buddies before they reached the end of kindergarten.

And after her parents' death, the gate had become more than just an easy access point to her best friend. It became her lifeline. Her gateway to belonging to something more than the little family she and her uncle could make. The residents on the Wright Ranch had always been so generous and welcoming to her. Without Caitlin and her family, Amanda wouldn't be the person she was today.

Liam pulled next to her and shouted over the ATVs' motors, "I'll get the gate." He accelerated and zoomed past her, stopping alongside the fence.

She slowed to a stop and waited for him to unlatch and swing the gate open. Liam might be the Neisson most likely to get into a fight at the drop of the hat, but he was still a gentleman.

"Thanks," she said as she drove through.

He tipped his hat in response.

As she waited for Liam to drive his ATV through and close the gate behind him, she gazed down into the shallow, narrow valley at the dark, wood-stained ranch house, horse barn with paddocks, outbuildings, and covered training arena that made up Sky High Ranch.

Her golden retriever, Honey, caught sight of them from her spot on the house's wraparound porch and started her mad tear up the rise to greet them.

Normally, she loved this view of her home. Today, all she saw were roofs that needed their missing and curled shingles repaired, buildings with paint curling at the edges and worn spots in the stain where the high desert sun, wind, and snow had battered the structures until the wood showed through and needed painting—

"We won't need this gate if Sky High becomes part of the Wright Ranch."

Liam's offhand sounding comment jolted Amanda out of her worrying. Did he mean they would make the fence unbroken, shutting her out because she would no longer be a welcomed neighbor, but a tenant? No, not tenants. She and her uncle would actually be employees if they agreed to stay on and manage Sky High as Thomas had suggested. Could she stomach that after fundamentally being treated as part of the family, at least when Caitlin had been home?

Did she have a choice?

No, she didn't. Not if she wanted to stay in her home.

Granted, she found herself spending more and more time

on the rodeo circuit, competing in as many barrel racing competitions both near and far as she could. She'd told herself it was the best way to market her barrel racer breeding program. But when her gaze caught on the scar cut into the land near the old equipment barn where her father had landed his small plane, a tiny voice whispered in her head that she'd simply been running away. How could she want to run away so much from a place that defined her so?

Liam eased his ATV next to hers.

His gaze tracked the same path as hers had, and she squirmed on the four-wheeler's seat as she imagined the catalog of faults he was mentally compiling. But when his attention seemed to stop on the stall paddock she had turned Whiskey Throttle out into this morning, her self-consciousness turned to anger. Did he really intend to report honestly to Thomas regarding the condition of her ranch, or would he simply say whatever would allow him to get his hands on her breeding stallion as quickly as possible?

Liam pulled his hat from his head and ran a hand through his sweat-darkened blond hair. "Looks like I have some roof repair in my future."

"What?"

He cut the engine on his ATV, as if thinking she hadn't been able to hear him. She'd heard him just fine. She'd simply assumed he'd been thinking about her horse.

"You're missing a ton of shingles." He pointed down at the buildings. "On the house, horse barn, and… well, all the out buildings. Fortunately, the pitches aren't as steep as at home."

She stared at him.

His brows went up. "You think I don't know how to swing a hammer?"

"Uh…" While she actually didn't believe there was anything Thomas Wright's grandchildren couldn't do if they set their minds to it, she'd assumed any work that needed to be done on the Wright Ranch was always hired out.

"There's no way my dad, let alone my grandfather, would have four boys hanging around the house without getting as much free labor out of us as possible. Trust me, there is nothing wrong with your ranch that I can't fix." He started his ATV again with a roar and prevented her from responding.

She wouldn't have. She knew, as well as anyone outside of the family, that those raised under Thomas Wright's roof had been raised in the cowboy way. But it was Liam's ability to accomplish what he set out to do that worried her. Because he seemed to have set his mind on acquiring her stallion for his breeding program.

She was going to have her work cut out for her finding a way to keep Whiskey Throttle.

★

OUT OF HABIT, Liam patted his pockets yet again for the little notebook and pen he already knew he'd forgotten in his distracted rush to join Amanda on her journey back to her ranch. He had to settle for recording the rapidly expanding list of repairs needed on the Sky High Ranch he was compiling on his cell phone. He wanted to be able to provide his grandfather with as complete and concise accounting as possible.

It didn't help his attention kept drifting to the big red stallion pacing in his paddock. Liam was itching to get a closer look at the big quarter horse.

And then there was the distraction that was Amanda. Liam was loath to admit she trumped all others. With her golden retriever, Honey, at her side, she'd shadowed his every move. Worry darkened her pretty brown eyes, making them seem even larger in her paler than normal face.

He was jolted by the realization of how accustomed he'd become to seeing her eyes sparkle with mischief. It bugged the hell out of him she thought he would take advantage of the situation. While he fully intended to do just that, at least to a certain extent, she was his little sister's best friend, for heaven's sake. He would never do her dirty.

It wasn't until it was nearly sunset that he realized she was no longer behind him, or hovering beside him, or directly in front of him as if trying to block his view of something she didn't want him to examine too closely. He'd spent God only knew how much time trying to get a decent picture with his phone of the drainage work that needed to be done in the front yard area between the house, stable, and gravel drive and hadn't noticed her leave. Now she was nowhere to be seen.

Liam straightened and slipped his phone into the back pocket of his jeans. She'd probably gone into the house for something. It struck him, despite knowing her a huge chunk of his life, he didn't have her phone number. He turned toward the low-slung ranch house, but didn't see any lights on within. Which didn't mean much, with the sun only just now slipping below the Cascade Mountains, painting the sky with a pink and orange hue, there was enough ambient light to see by.

Making this the perfect time to get a closer look at Whiskey Throttle before it was too dark to see anything of importance. There was no point hounding Amanda about the stallion if the horse turned out to not be what Liam needed for his bucking bronc breeding program, after all. Something he wouldn't know for sure until he was able to get a good look at the animal, and the light was quickly fading.

Taking one last glance toward the house, which called to him in a way he'd never experienced, Liam headed toward the stable. He supposed he'd grown far too used to being hounded by haunting memories at the Wright Ranch.

With extended eaves and cedar-plank siding stained dark like the ranch house, the stable had two rows of stalls separated by a wide, paved walkway and two sets of sliding doors at either end. Each stall opened on the inside to the walkway as well as its own paddock extending outward from the stable.

While lacking the heating and air-conditioning, not to mention the brass fittings and elaborate woodwork and lighting of the Wright Ranch stables, it was very clean and well maintained—aside from the missing roof shingles and faded stain.

Still not spotting Amanda, Liam skirted the stable on the side he'd earlier noticed Whiskey Throttle to be paddocked.

While the other horses confined to the stable had reentered their stalls to eat their evening meals Amanda had provided them with already, the big roan stallion was still pacing the length of the far paddock. Liam's breath caught. Amanda was right to be possessive of her new horse. The tall, broad-chested stud was gorgeous, with a shiny reddish-brown coat and mane that glinted even in the fading light. And the way the horse tossed his head and spun on his back hooves every time he reached the confines of his split-rail pen spoke of a spirit that did not take to being contained.

Oh, yeah. Liam wanted him badly.

Whiskey made another circuit of his paddock then paused at the end, his well-shaped head high and ears pricked toward Liam. Blowing a loud, wet snort, the horse swung his attention to the open field beyond the stable.

That was when Liam saw her. Amanda was sitting cross-legged on the ground, facing away from the stable, the late summer grass moving like ocean waves around her. Her dog lay next to her.

The wind lifted her dark brown hair and he noticed, for the first time today, her hair was frizzed and wild, not its normal perfect silky curls. It occurred to him she hadn't been made up, either. She was such a fresh-faced beauty he hadn't noticed the lack of eye shadow or gloss.

There was something about the way she sat with her hand buried in Honey's blond fur, her back bowed and her head slightly down, that drew Liam to her. He didn't like seeing her looking so defeated.

He walked right past the horse he'd been wanting to see all day, his focus glued to the woman he was so used to seeing taking on the world with her head held high, her hair and makeup done to perfection. Had the reality of losing her family's ranch, her home, finally hit her?

Empathy twisted in his gut.

But if he was able to do the needed repairs and his grandfather bought the place, she and her uncle wouldn't have to leave. Nothing would really change for her.

The urge to reassure her, to comfort her, seized him. He wanted to make her see everything would be okay.

Though his booted steps crunched loudly in the dry grass, she didn't turn when he approached. Nor did she turn toward him when he lowered himself to the ground and took a seat next to her and the dog, stretching his legs out in front of him.

He studied Amanda, struck again by how pretty she was. Had she always been?

Her gaze was fixed on a spot in front of them. The grass grew sparsely there, and he realized it look similar for about twenty or thirty feet and extended in either direction for the length of a couple football fields.

Understanding slammed into him. She was staring at the homemade landing strip her father had cut into the earth for his small, single-prop airplane.

The airplane he and her mom had lost their lives in when it crashed into a faraway mountain one snowy night.

The muscles in his chest tightened. Bending his legs, he

dug his boot heels into the ground and propped his elbows atop his knees. "Thinking about your folks?"

She glanced at him, pain swirled into the rich chocolate brown of her eyes. Her lips flattened and she quickly flicked her gaze away from his, back to the landing strip in front of them. "No. Not at all."

Yeah, right. Liam suppressed a snort. He couldn't remember exactly how old Amanda had been when her parents died, but she hadn't been very big. He had distinct memories of a little dark-haired girl with big, sad eyes seemingly becoming a fixture in his lone sister's life. Clearly she was still haunted by her parents' death.

If there was one thing Liam knew a thing or two about, it was haunting memories.

While he wanted to be left the hell alone when the past clawed at his innards, he couldn't bear to leave Amanda to drown in her pain. After hesitating a heartbeat or two, he lifted an arm and slid it around her shoulders. Though she was more than capable of bucking hay and controlling twelve hundred pounds of hyper barrel racer, she felt slight and delicate beneath his arm.

He was debating if he dare draw her closer when she collapsed against him. He instantly wrapped her in both arms. She fit so perfectly against him. Tenderness welled inside him, startling and complete.

Her gaze collided with his, and the shadow of pain—and loneliness—darkening her brown eyes tugged hard on the part of him he worked zealously to conceal.

Then her gaze dropped to his mouth, and before he

could form the thought, he was kissing her.

Kissing Amanda Rodrigues, his little sister's best friend.

And he'd never felt anything so good in his life.

CHAPTER FOUR

Just because Liam knew he shouldn't be kissing Amanda didn't mean he wanted to stop.

The moment his mouth contacted hers the sunset faded away. The gently swaying grass surrounding them disappeared. The scar in the earth that used to be Amanda's father's landing strip lost its power to hurt. Liam had thought the electricity that had arched through him the moment he'd touched his lips to hers was the best thing he'd ever felt in his life.

Until she kissed him back.

Being lassoed and dragged behind a galloping horse through gravel would have less of an impact on his composure.

She slid her lips along his, then opened her mouth to him, touching her tongue to his. He groaned, the contact gripping him in the pit of his gut.

This was madness. He couldn't be doing this. Not with her. This wasn't why his grandfather had sent him here. He was supposed to be finding ways to help her, not take advantage of her sorrow.

He reached up to take a hold of both sides of her face,

intending to gently ease her back away from him, but the moment his fingers touched her satiny skin he found himself sliding his hands into her long dark hair and pulling her closer. He'd dreamt of her hair after she galloped past him in the rodeo arena, chasing down his escaped bronc.

One of her small hands found his whisker-roughened cheek then skimmed to the back of his neck, trailing fire in its wake, while the other settled over his pounding heart like a hot brand.

He'd never felt this sort of intensity with a simple kiss. And he'd had plenty of opportunities. He admittedly played the field fast and loose, but he never let any woman get too close. But here, now, he wanted Amanda close. Very close.

The feel of her, the way she tasted, was so right.

And so wrong.

He was a better man than this. He'd promised his mother on her deathbed he'd be a better man. But he couldn't stop kissing her.

An ear-splitting, panicked whinny from Whiskey Throttle jerked him out of the thrall her mouth had snared him within.

He and Amanda pulled back from each other in the same instant, their hands dropping away from where they'd been touching. They both twisted to look behind them toward the red stallion in his paddock. The horse was tossing his head and half-rearing in clear agitation. Amanda's other horses that she had currently stabled, including the ever-steady Rumbles, left their stalls and their evening meals to pace the confines of their paddocks. Rumbles whinnied repeatedly, her nose high and her ears flattened.

Honey lifted her nose and began to bark.

Amanda turned toward him, and he met her troubled gaze. They both rose to their feet.

She asked, "What's going on?"

"So, this isn't normal?" he asked, even though he already knew it wasn't.

He knew the sound of panicked horses when he heard it. He automatically scanned the ground near the horses for sign of a western rattle snake. While not as common as in some areas, the snake was native to Central Oregon.

"Not even close." Her worry was clear in the tightness of her voice and the darkening of her deep brown eyes.

They started walking toward the stable. He turned and watched Rumbles run the length of her paddock then back again. This was the same horse who'd brought Amanda within arm's length of an out-of-control bronc without so much as a flick of an ear. Something had to be seriously wrong to send the mare into such an agitated state. "What do you think has them so spooked?"

Amanda looked around. "I don't—" Her nostrils flared and her eyes widened.

Liam smelled it, too. Smoke.

He started to run the same time Amanda did, his gaze jumping to the stable's roofline vents, windows, and doors. They ran into the stable, looking everywhere. Nothing. No sign of smoke at all. Thank God. But that didn't explain the distinct, acrid smell of something on fire. They walked back out of the stable.

Amanda said, "Do you think it's a prescribed burn somewhere?"

"Not this time of year. It would be too dangerous and difficult to control with everything so dry." The high desert of Central Oregon routinely had long, hot summers with very little rainfall and this year had not been an exception.

He looked toward the ridge of mountains dominating the western horizon, looking for telltale smoke silhouetted against the sunset. "But it could be a forest fire." They weren't that far from the forests of the Central Oregon Cascade Mountains. Fire, either sparked by lightning or man-made, was a fact of life.

The wind shifted, sending the knee-high yellow grass stalks dancing toward the stables, and the smell of smoke became stronger. Undeniable. The horses' agitation grew in response. His stomach clenched and his entire body went on high alert.

He and Amanda turned simultaneously toward the smell.

"There," Amanda said and pointed the same instant Liam spotted the smoke in the pasture they'd crossed when traveling from the Wright Ranch to Sky High. The smoke, organizing into a single column spiraling upward, was barely visible in the fading light. But the fire beneath, glowing red and pulsing in sync with the wind as it devoured the grass, was clearly visible.

Had the heat from the ATVs' engines or exhaust pipes ignited the tinder-dry grass as they passed over it? *Damn.* He should have known better. They should have driven a truck the short distance on the road. Thank goodness they'd been sitting outside and were alerted to the fire before it became all consuming.

Amanda looked toward the sky, the setting sun turning the smoke a vibrant orange red. "How?" Clearly, she was looking for evidence of a possible lightning strike and was finding none.

"We'll worry about the *how* later. We need to put this out. Do you have a water truck?"

"No," she replied on a scoff that reminded him this wasn't the Wright Ranch.

His grandfather kept their ranch equipped with every piece of machinery that could ever be needed on a large, profitable rodeo stock contractor ranch.

"But Uncle Red has a one-hundred-gallon water tank with a pump mounted in the back of his old pickup truck."

"Please tell me that's not what he drove when he left for Calgary."

Amanda turned and started to run toward the barn, her golden retriever charging after her. "Of course not," she called over her shoulder. "It would have never made it to Canada."

Taking one last look toward the fire, noting grimly that the red glow was definitely becoming larger and more visible in the fading light, he sprinted after Amanda. He pulled his cell phone from his pocket as he ran. They would need help.

When he reached the barn, Amanda glanced at him as she heaved one side of the sliding barn door open. "911?"

"No. Ian. Who'll get Drew if he's around, as well as anyone else who is handy." He slid the other side of the door open with his free hand as he hit the autodial for his oldest brother. "They'll get here faster with our big water truck than the fire department could with their pump truck."

"Good thinking. Thanks." She ran inside, hitting the lights in the utilitarian but tidy barn.

It struck him how in control she seemed, but he reminded himself she was a cowgirl, born and raised, and undoubtedly knew panic never helped anyone. It certainly hadn't helped him save his mother. Panic had frozen him to the spot, awash with terror, outside of the corral where his mom had been trampled. He'd vowed to never feel that helpless ever again.

As he connected with Ian and told him succinctly about the fire and what they needed, Amanda darted to a row of hooks on the wall where several sets of keys to the various vehicles and farm equipment parked inside the barn were hung. She snatched a set of keys threaded on a ring that also sported a once-white rabbit's foot.

He'd take that as an omen. They could definitely use all the luck they could get. Ending his call with Ian, he held out his hand for her to toss him the keys.

She palmed them instead. "I'll drive. Betty is finicky." To the dog, she said, "Honey, stay!"

The retriever immediately dropped to her butt, looking between the two of them with her tongue dangling from the side of her mouth.

Amanda ran to the driver's side of an ancient pickup truck that had once been white, like the rabbit's foot, but was now mostly rust. Thankfully, it was parked in front of the hay cutter and bailer, not behind it or the six-horse trailer, or tractor that were in the other row of vehicles in the big barn. The time it would have taken them to move any of the vehicles out of the way would have cost them their chance to contain the grass fire.

He squelched the spurt of annoyance at her for not letting him drive and focused on the absurd, instead. "Betty?" he asked as he climbed into the passenger's side of the truck and settled on the cracked bench seat.

She took a seat behind the wheel. "Yeah. Betty." She slammed her door shut, inserted the key, and started the engine with a surprisingly robust roar. "As in Betty… Boop." She hit the gear shift into drive with more of a smack than a boop and stomped on the gas, propelling them out of the barn with a spray of gravel, dirt, and straw.

She didn't let up on the gas as she careened around the stable, sending the horses hightailing back into their stalls. She only slowed slightly to navigate the thankfully open gate near the stable in the fence surrounding the burning pasture, then floored it again and sent them bouncing toward the fire.

In the time it had taken them to get the truck the fire had spread to the fence separating their ranches, and with the additional fuel of the treated wood of the fence the smoke had turned thick, black and oily. His mouth went dry.

He asked, "How long is the hose?"

"Not long."

He ground his teeth. "Then get close. As close as you can."

"I know," she responded tartly, and parked much closer

than he would have, where the smoke was thickest. But they had to get ahead of its spread, which meant being downwind of the choking smoke.

The moment the truck stopped they both bailed out. Liam pulled his hat off and tossed it back in the truck's cab, then uncoiled the hose and opened the spout, stepping practically into the flames. Amanda climbed into the bed and started working the lever to pump the water from the tank into the hose. At first the water flowed steady and strong, allowing him to extinguish the flames closest to him and wet the yet unburned grass. But it didn't take long for the flow of water to diminish. He looked back at Amanda and instantly recognized she was struggling to maintain the pace needed to hand-pump the water from the tank.

"Amanda, switch with me!" Why hadn't he realized she didn't have the strength or endurance to work the pump for long?

"No! I've got this."

Because she was too stubborn and proud to ever admit she couldn't do what needed to be done, that was why. But instead of being annoyed with her, admiration exploded in his chest as he ignored her and headed for the back of Betty.

"Switch!" he insisted, setting the hose nozzle on the back gate and climbing into the truck bed. Knowing full well how physically demanding running one of these pumps was, he stripped down to his undershirt, tossing his shirt into the corner of the truck bed.

Amanda made a noise reminiscent of his sister Caitlin. Neither women liked to be told they couldn't do something.

But clearly valuing her ranch more than her pride, she left her spot at the pump handle and jumped from the truck bed. Taking the hose and nozzle in hand, she hurried to where he'd been standing. Much too close to the hot, crackling red flames dancing in the wind.

"No! Not there. Move back."

"This is exactly where you were standing!"

"I know. And you're too close. Move back, Amanda."

She turned and grinned up at him. "So you're saying you were doing something stupid?"

"Amanda…" Now was not the time.

The thought of her getting burned made his chest tight. He started pumping water from the tank so she'd have to focus on what they were doing. And to give her the ability to protect herself. If something happened to her on his watch… the thought sent a chill down his spine.

But she protected herself handily, knocking down the flames at her feet with an effective back and forth motion.

A deep rumble of a huge engine downshifting heralded the arrival of the Wright Ranch's four-thousand-gallon water truck. It crested the small hill where the gate in the fence between the properties was located. Drew's pickup truck, loaded with four of their ranch hands, arrived close behind.

With the fence itself now on fire, the water truck, driven by Thomas Wright himself with Liam's father next to him, pulled alongside the fence and released a heavy spray of water from the side spouts normally used for dust control in the arenas. Liam wasn't surprised that both his dad and grandfather had come to help. Fire was no joke on any ranching property, let alone one running a highly sought after and thus profitable rodeo rough stock operation.

Drew, Ian, and the ranch hands spilled from the pickup truck, some with shovels which they immediately employed burying the flames and smoldering grass in scoops of dirt. Ian and Drew ran to the back of the water truck and pulled a large hose from its storage tube and worked together to attach it to a spout on the truck. Ian then took control of the other end of the hose as Drew opened the valve to release a spray of water ten times stronger than what he and Amanda were producing.

His dad climbed from the truck and yelled, "Are you two okay?"

Liam glanced at Amanda, still stubbornly standing too close to the fire's edge but making clear progress in knocking down the fire in front of her. Without slowing his pumping, despite the burn steadily building in his arms, shoulders, and back, he yelled, "Yeah, we're good."

From where he stood on the other side of the fence, Ian shouted over the water truck's engine and the gushing water, "Amanda! Take two steps back away from those flames. Caitlin will kill us if we let you burn your hair off before her wedding."

Amanda nearly dropped the water hose in her haste to step precisely two steps back and pat at her hair on the off-chance it had indeed caught on fire.

While there was no doubt Ian possessed the ability to keep Caitlin and Amanda in line, there was obviously nothing like the threat of being the cause of a bad wedding photo to conquer Amanda's stubbornness. Why hadn't Liam thought of it?

With Amanda's imminent safety no longer his chief motivator, the burn in Liam's muscles became difficult to ignore. But as long as Amanda stood in harm's way, he'd be damned if he'd stop.

He could examine why later.

★

THE WATER PRESSURE in the hose faltered for the first time since Liam had taken over pumping the water from the pickup-mounted tank. Amanda glanced toward where he stood in the pickup bed furiously working the pump handle that forced the water from the large plastic tank to the hose she held. While Liam's pace pumping the handle hadn't decreased, the force he exerted clearly had. Concern arced through her.

The amount of sweat streaming down his face and the veins popping from his bulging muscles made her worry he had to be reaching his limits. But there was no way he would cede to her.

Squinting through the smoke, she sought Drew. She spotted him scooping heaping shovelfuls of dirt onto the leading edge of the fire on the Sky High Ranch side of the fence. Granted, he was only a couple years younger than her, he vibrated with the enthusiasm of youth.

"Drew!" she yelled.

He stopped mid-shovel and met her gaze through the

haze of smoke.

She lifted her chin toward Liam, counting on a near lifetime of familiarity for him to comprehend her meaning.

He shouldered the shovel handle and tugged at the bill of his ball cap.

Message received.

Continuing to soak the now sputtering flames in front of her, she surreptitiously watched her best friend's second youngest brother climb into Betty's bed and approach Caitlin's second oldest—and reputedly scariest—brother. The brother Amanda had been engaged in the most toe-curling kiss she'd ever experienced before the fire interrupted them.

Good God.

She'd never been kissed like that before. Even Joe, her high school boyfriend who'd broken her heart by leaving her behind along with the small town cowboy life, had never kissed her like that.

Not surprisingly, Liam initially shook Drew off, but then Liam's gaze rose to hers. His blue eyes locked on to hers. She didn't need to be fighting a fire to feel like she was about to go up in flames. But she held her ground.

She willed him to give over to Drew, to cut himself some slack and take a much needed break.

He surprised her by doing just that, straightening with obvious discomfort and gesturing for Drew to take command of the pump from him. After picking up the shovel Drew had set down in the bed, Liam jumped from the back of Betty and strode toward her. His long legs ate up the distance and his soot-streaked white undershirt stuck to his muscled chest with sweat. Amanda had thought her heart couldn't beat any faster than when they'd raced to the fire. She was wrong.

He propped the shovel against the truck and reached for the hose. When she resisted, he tugged it from her grasp. "Get back in the truck, Amanda. We've got this."

Amanda gritted her teeth. She might have let Liam kiss her, and she might let him do it again, but she'd be damned if she'd let him tell her what to do.

CHAPTER FIVE

THE BELLIGERENT JUT of Amanda's jaw, lit from below by the smoldering grass fire, should have been enough to make Liam rephrase his request for Amanda to wait in the truck. And when Drew barked out a laugh and said, "Way to step in it, bro," he knew he'd said the wrong thing. But there was no way he was going to back down now.

He told himself it was because Caitlin would indeed kill him if he allowed Amanda, Caitlin's maid of honor, to be singed in any way so close to the wedding.

In the rodeoing world, there was only a small window of downtime—after the nationals in Vegas in December and before the circuits started up again after the first of the year—and Caitlin and Bodie had scheduled their wedding to happen in the narrow time frame. But their engagement party was set for this Saturday at the Wright Ranch. And she was working herself into a tizzy about it because of the dynamics of the two families involved. Nothing like a long-standing feud to make an upcoming wedding interesting.

But as much as he wanted to blame his concern on Caitlin's potential wrath, the thought of Amanda hurt in any way brought a heavy, sick feeling to the pit of his stomach. He'd grown up with her like a brother, after all. But when his gaze dropped to her mouth, the memory of their kiss was like a shovel to the back of his knees.

He was so full of horseshit.

Amanda readjusted her grip on the hose and nozzle as Drew began rebuilding the pressure in the line by working the handle on the pump.

She sent Liam a hard glare in the fading light. "This is my ranch, Liam. At least for now. And those are my horses down there." She glanced toward the stable down the rise where the sound of nervous whinnies still reached them. "You can't honestly expect me to wait in the truck when even a single blade of grass is still on fire."

"Yeah, honestly, Liam," Drew interjected from the truck bed.

"Shut it, Drew," Liam said without taking his gaze from Amanda. Why did she have to be so stubborn?

Before he could think of another tact to take with her, Ian shouted from the fence line over the noise of the water tanker engine, "Liam, move that truck so we can run the tanker past that area." Ian then rushed to uncouple the hose he'd been using so the truck could knock down what remained of the fire with the spray nozzles mounted all around the tanker truck.

"Will do," Liam called back with a wave in case he couldn't be heard, then turned back to Amanda. "Please." He held out a hand. "Let me help you."

She heaved a sigh and handed over the nozzle to him. Relief and an undeniable satisfaction flooded him as he shut off the water hose nozzle.

Drew, having obviously heard Ian, had stopped pumping and started pulling the hose back into the pickup truck bed. Liam turned and tossed the nozzle up to Drew to secure in the bed as Amanda retrieved the shovel and stowed it in the pickup truck bed as well.

Liam opened the truck's passenger door and held it wide for Amanda. She made a noise, the one he was becoming to know well, and climbed into the truck cab. Halfway expecting her to slide across the bench seat to sit behind the wheel, he hurried around the front of the battered old truck to the driver's side and climbed in.

Very aware of Amanda sitting next to him, he started Betty's engine and gave the gear shifter the requisite "boop" to move the transmission from park to drive. Feeling stupidly victorious for successfully conquering the test that was Betty Boob, he drove the truck just far enough away from the smoldering grass fire to allow his grandfather to maneuver the large water tanker over the area that needed to be soaked. He turned Betty toward the fire, though, so the old pickup truck's headlights could illuminate the area along with the tanker and the headlights and rack-mounted lights on Drew's truck that he'd left on.

As soon as Liam stopped Betty, Drew grabbed up the shovel and jumped from the truck bed. He joined two of the Wright Ranch hands digging a fire line downslope from the fire.

Amanda reached for the passenger door handle, but Liam stayed her with a hand on her nearest forearm.

"Let the water truck do its work." There was no way Grandfather would let the fire spread.

Amanda sent him a look he couldn't decipher in the darkening cab, but she relaxed back into the cracked bench seat and turned her attention to watching his grandfather drive the water truck through the gate in the fence separating the two ranch properties.

As soon as the big tanker cleared the gate, though, Grandfather stopped the rig and climbed out from the cab along with Dad. Grandfather gestured for Drew to come to him. Drew handed off his shovel to Big Mike, one the ranch hands, and climbed into the tanker truck's cab and took over driving it slowly along the edge of the fire, rapidly soaking it into oblivion and wetting the surrounding grass.

His grandfather, dad, and oldest brother walked along the Sky High Ranch side of the fence near the gate, their gazes down as they kicked at the still smoldering grass.

A sinking, sick weight settled in Liam's gut. Having driven his ATV through that gate and right over that grass just hours ago, Liam had to know what they were saying.

"Wait here," he told Amanda without thinking as he opened the driver's door, grabbed his hat, and hopped out.

"Stop telling me what to do, Neisson," she grouched right before he slammed the truck door shut.

Despite the gnawing fear he'd set the place on fire, a smile tugged at his mouth. Damn, he liked her spunk. Figuring she'd be fast on his heels despite what he'd told her to do, he put his hat on his head and didn't wait for her. He headed straight toward the other men silhouetted at the fence in Drew's truck lights, stomping on smoldering clumps of grass as he went.

God help him if he'd started this fire.

As if kissing Amanda hadn't been bad enough.

★

AMANDA'S FINGERS CURLED around the cold metal of the door handle as Betty's interior light clicked off. She kept her gaze focused on Liam's broad back, his strength of body and will obvious in every purposeful step he took. A strength that was all the more alluring because she knew what had shaped it.

Knew it and understood it.

She had firsthand experience with the sort of life events that forced a person to harden or shatter beneath the pain.

And now that they'd kissed…

She found herself wanting to smooth the sharp edges of his past.

With a strength of will of her own, she shut down the hot flush of yearning the memory of his mouth on hers sent through her, wiped at a strand of hair stuck to her cheek, and yanked the truck door handle and opened the door. The only thing she should be thinking about was how to save what her parents had built.

She trudged in Liam's trail through the sloppy mess created by partially burnt, trampled, and now drenched grass with the rapidly forming mud beneath. She followed him up the rise to the charred fence line where the elder members of his family had gathered.

A small flashlight in hand, Ian had squatted down and was picking at something in the grass. His father and grandfather were standing close, directing Ian's search.

The noise created by the tanker truck prevented her from hearing what Liam said to them when he reached them, or what they were saying in return. But she saw Liam pull his phone from his jeans' pocket and take a picture of whatever Ian was pointing at, the flash illuminating the group of handsome, compelling men in a blaze of white light.

There was no denying how fortunate she was to have these men come to her aid. She shoved aside the knowledge that their ranch, and thus their ample livelihood, lay only a now-smoldering fence away.

Douglas Neisson glanced up at her approach. Besides Uncle Red, Caitlin's dad had been the closest thing to a father Amanda had known. At least as much of a father figure as he could be in his own grief after the love of his life had been terribly injured by a rampaging bull. Injuries she eventually died from.

Pointing at whatever his two oldest boys were studying, he said, "I'm assuming you haven't picked up a new bad habit, little miss."

"What?" She moved closer to see what he was talking about.

Liam turned to her, his scowl fiercer than normal with only half of his face and hat illuminated by the lights on Drew's truck. "I told you to stay in the truck." His tone, a mix of frustration and resignation, said he wasn't the slightest bit surprised to find her standing next to him.

She was pretty sure everyone but her and Liam chuckled as only grown men could.

A very warm, decidedly fuzzy feeling infused her at the knowledge these men knew her. Really knew her. Maybe she wasn't as alone as she'd thought she was with Uncle Red gone.

"Could it be Red's?" Ian asked.

She stepped closer, trying to see what had them so intrigued.

All she saw was burned grass and mud. "What are you talking about?"

Ian used his small mag light to push aside a clump of burnt grass then directed the beam of light at something in the mud.

Amanda leaned closer until she spotted the singed remains of three cigarettes.

She snapped upright and met Liam's gaze. His eyes glowed so clear a blue in the headlights of Drew's truck that her breath caught in her throat, but the hard set of his jaw refocused her.

It was one thing to believe they had accidently started the fire with the hot undercarriage or exhaust pipes of their ATVs, but to discover the grass had been ignited by such blatant careless disregard was something else entirely.

"No. Neither Uncle Red nor I smoke. Anything," she said, glancing back to Douglas with his hands buried in his front pockets and Thomas, who stood with his arms crossed over his barrel chest and his face shadowed by his cowboy hat pulled low. With the fire all but extinguished, she was compelled to try to lighten the mood. "Chew, on the other hand…"

Liam grabbed her elbow. "You use chewing tobacco?"

His fingers were hot but his grip was gentle. The memory of him skimming his fingers across her cheeks and into her hair derailed her momentarily.

She blinked to refocus. "No. Of course not." She'd never make it onto another rodeo royal court if she did. And her parents would not have approved.

Ian shifted on his haunches to look up at his brother. "When was the last time you talked to Old Red? That's not his cud he's always chewing on, you know."

Liam slid his fingers from her arm with what she thought was reluctance. Her heart bumped in her chest.

Liam crossed his arms like his grandfather. "It's hard to tell anything with that beard of his."

"Regardless," Thomas said, putting an end to the silly chew discussion. "With only you and Red working Sky High, that rules out the smoker being from this side of the fence." He looked hard at Ian. "I trust that no one employed at the Wright Ranch smokes cigarettes, and even if they did, that they wouldn't be foolish enough to discard their butts anywhere near such dry grass."

"No rancher or cowboy would," Douglas said, probably hoping to take some of the heat off his oldest, who'd taken over as the general manager of the Wright Ranch roughly two years ago. He pulled a red-and-black bandanna from his back pocket and handed it to Liam.

"So, who did?" Liam said as he used the bandanna to collect the butts.

Uncertainty coiling and uncoiling in her stomach, Amanda asked, "Do you really think that's what started the fire?"

Ian straightened, carefully wrapping the cigarette butts within the square of cloth. "I'm no expert, but judging how blackened the grass is right in this area"—he pointed to the badly burnt clumps fanning out from where the cigarette butts had been—"odds are good the fire started here. And as dry as it's been, it really would only take one still burning cigarette, let alone three, to ignite the grass."

Amanda's uncertainty fermented into something akin to fear as she looked down the fifty feet or so of fence line illuminated by the trucks' headlights. While anything beyond the reach of the headlights was fully swallowed by darkness, about a half mile down lay the county road from which the gravel drive to Sky High branched off from and that ultimately led to the paved, and gated, drive to the Wright Ranch. Only acres and acres of pasture land lay in the opposite direction from where they stood on the fence line. The odds of anyone coming from a direction other than the road or the Wright Ranch were very, very thin.

She or Liam would have seen the smoker if the person had reached this spot from her ranch. After all, she had been following Liam around outside just down the slope on her side of the fence for the majority of the day. While she'd admittedly been focused on Liam and what he'd been doing right up until she'd escaped to the back pasture, she was certain she would have noticed anyone driving up to her ranch and wandering around smoking cigarettes.

Still, she met Liam's gaze. "Did you see anyone along the fence line today?"

"I didn't." He reached up, as if intending to touch her face, but stopped, his hand dropping back to his side.

"Liam," Ian said, drawing Liam's attention. Ian gestured toward the open gate in the fence. The two men walked together toward it, out of Amanda's hearing.

Her curiosity flared as quickly and as hot as the fire had in the tinder-dry grass. She turned to follow.

"Come here, my girl," Caitlin's father said, stopping her, his arms spread wide.

No matter how much she wanted to know what Ian was saying to Liam, she would never, ever, pass on a hug from Caitlin's father. He'd retreated so completely from everyday life after Caitlin's mother's accident and eventual death that any outreach from him was like a ray of warm sunlight on a gray winter day.

She went to him and stepped into his arms. Everything settled and became calm when he wrapped her in his embrace.

"Are you all right?" he asked.

Her ruff would have instantly gone up if anyone else had asked her the same question, seemingly doubting her ability to handle such a crisis. However, Douglas would never doubt her abilities. Caitlin thought her dad patronized her, but Amanda had never felt anything other than a sincere concern from him.

One of her clearest memories after her parents' deaths was Douglas drawing her onto his lap in front of the huge fireplace in the Wright Ranch main house and telling her stories about what an amazing horsewoman her mother had been and how proud she would be of Amanda. Red had done the same thing, but hearing it from Douglas had been more powerful, somehow. Probably because Douglas hadn't been obligated to comfort the little orphan girl.

Now, she pulled in a smoke-tinged lungful of his woodsy sent that had never changed in all these years and nodded against his shoulder. "I'm okay."

"That's my girl." He eased her away from him, then frowned and turned her until the headlights from at least one of the trucks fell onto her face and made her squint against the bright light. He *tsked* and licked the pad of his thumb then used it to wipe at her cheek. "God help us if this doesn't just wash off."

Thomas waved a dismissive hand. "Leave her be. Caitlin will be fine with a smudge or two. What won't wash off will wear off in time for the wedding. Burnt hair, on the other hand…" He trailed off and turned away to watch the progress of Drew in the tanker truck and his ranch hands using their shovels to smother any remaining smoldering grass with wet grass and mud.

Amanda grabbed at her hair in terror.

"It's fine, Amanda. You're fine. Nothing a hot shower won't fix." Douglas patted at her shoulder and released her, shifting his attention to his two eldest children still talking at the gate. "Liam," he called.

Liam acknowledge his father with a gesture, said something else to Ian, who patted his shoulder in acknowledgement and headed off toward Drew's truck. Liam turned and walked toward them. "Yeah?"

Douglas said, "I want you to stay close to Amanda until we get to the bottom of this."

Thomas nodded. "I agree. Until Red returns."

"Already planned on it," Liam said and wrapped a hand around her upper arm.

Why did she think of his touch as being more of a caress than a controlling grip? Because she'd had a day, that was why.

She shrugged her arm free of his hold. To Douglas, she said, "I told you I'm okay."

"I know you are, my girl. But now I'll be."

Amanda opened her mouth then immediately snapped it shut. She couldn't argue that. She steadied herself with a deep breath. Having Liam on her ranch, in her space, for one day was bad enough. Now he was to stay with her for heaven knew how long? Great. Just great.

She wrapped her arms around her middle and turned to watch Drew drive the tanker truck through the middle of the burned patch. The spray nozzles mounted on the sides and back of the tanker drenched either side thoroughly as well as squashing any remaining embers beneath the truck's massive tires, squishing them into the deepening mud.

When he reached them, Drew shut off the water and rolled down the driver's side window. "Do you think we got it?" he called to his dad and grandfather.

Thomas Wright scanned the flattened, scorched patch of grass and the fencing alongside it.

Amanda followed his gaze with hers, trying as well to spot a glow of ember or hint of sizzle that would reveal a hot spot with the potential to reignite the surrounding unburnt dry grass. She saw none. As far as she could tell, they'd successfully put out the fire. Relief flooded her.

Apparently drawing the same conclusion, Thomas gave a sharp nod of his head and turned to walk back through the gate toward Drew's truck.

Douglas put two fingers to his lips and gave a sharp whistle, drawing the ranch hands' attention. "That's good, boys. Load up."

Their shovels in hand, the men made their way back to the gate, stomping on or overturning apparently suspicious clumps of grass as they went.

Amanda thanked each of them as they went by, truly grateful for their efforts. Liam tugged the brim of his hat, high praise from him.

To Drew, Douglas said, "You good driving that through the gate?"

Drew scoffed. "Yes, of course."

His dad saluted him in acknowledgment. "Hang on a sec, and I'll ride with you." He returned his attention to Liam. "I'll feel better knowing you'll check on this"—he waved a hand at the blackened patch of earth—"in a couple of hours. Sooner if the wind picks up. And at least once again during the night."

"Will do."

"I can give you a wakeup call if you think you'll need it."

Liam glanced at her. "I don't think there will be much sleeping happening tonight."

CHAPTER SIX

A HOT FLUSH flooded Amanda's cheeks. How could Liam tell his father they wouldn't be sleeping tonight? She fisted her hands to keep from smacking him. Did he think just because they'd kissed she'd let him into her bed? Just because she'd fantasized—more than once—about making love with the big oaf didn't mean she was going to just throw the sheets back. Even though the mere thought of being tangled in the sheets with Liam made her all hot and tingly.

She had to get a grip.

His dad reached out to pat them both on the shoulder. "I don't think there's any real cause for worry. Everything will be fine."

Amanda's embarrassment doubled. Of course Douglas wouldn't take Liam's comment to mean there would be anything physical going on between them. Why would he? Liam had never given her the time of day in the past. He seemed to prefer leggy blondes who didn't care that he didn't call them back.

So, why had he kissed her?

Douglas gave Liam one last pat. "Do text or call me after

you've checked the fence and surrounding grass, though."

So much for his *everything will be fine* spiel. A chilling sense of foreboding gripped Amanda. Okay, Liam spending the night at her ranch wasn't such a bad thing, after all.

"I will, Dad. See you later," Liam said solemnly.

He was clearly taking the situation seriously, also. He lifted a hand toward where his grandfather sat waiting in Drew's truck.

"Thank you for your help, Mr. Neisson." Amanda gave Douglas a quick hug.

"Of course, Amanda. We're always here for you." He chucked her under the chin with his knuckle like he used to when she was little then walked to the passenger side of the tanker truck and climbed in.

From the driver's side, Drew said, "I have a go-bag in my truck you can use. Unless you want to spend the night in what you have on."

Liam glanced down at his wet, muddy, and smoke saturated jeans and undershirt. "Uh, no. Thanks, man."

Drew saluted them before putting the huge truck into gear. Liam snagged her elbow again and eased her out of the way as if not entirely trusting his younger brother's driving skills or her ability to avoid having her foot run over. She tried to ignore his warm fingers and focus on his high-handedness and the tanker truck slowly making its way through the gate. One of the Wright Ranch hands closed, or at least tried to close, the gate behind the tanker. Both the fence post the gate was hinged on as well as the post it latched to were no longer entirely vertical, either due to the fire or, more likely, the water-softened earth allowing them to lean.

Liam released her and jogged up to the gate to help the hand wrestle it shut. The best they could do was prop the gate against the latch-side post. He gestured toward Drew's truck, and the ranch hand trotted over to the tricked-out club cab pickup. One of the guys already inside tossed out a small duffel bag which the hand easily caught and ran back to Liam. He handed the duffel over the fence to Liam then hustled back to the pickup. With everyone on board, Thomas drove the pickup in the wake of the tanker truck down the slope toward the Wright Ranch.

With only Betty's age-yellowed headlights illuminating the field now, the night closed in with a foreboding oppressiveness. The normal spray of stars that would blanket the sky on moonless nights like this were nowhere to be found, undoubtedly obscured by lingering smoke. Suddenly feeling vulnerable in a way she never had before on this ranch, she waited for Liam to return with Drew's duffel before she started toward Red's old truck.

She pointed at the duffel when he reached her. "A go-bag?"

"Yeah, for emergencies. You grab your bag and go. Grandfather insists everybody has one packed and stashed somewhere. It's no great shocker Drew keeps his in his truck."

"So, his is more of an overnight bag."

Liam gave a short laugh. "Pretty much."

"Where's yours?" To her knowledge, unlike Drew, Liam

didn't have much of a social life, other than his serial dating. His time was primarily spent obsessively focused on his broncs and the ranch.

"In the horse barn."

He confirmed her suspicion. "Why am I not surprised?" No way would he bug out without seeing to his horses. Something they had in common.

They reached Betty and he tossed the bag into the back then went to the passenger side and got in. Apparently, with the threat literally extinguished, he didn't feel the need for control. So annoying.

She climbed behind the wheel. "Fingers crossed the battery isn't dead after having just the lights on for so long."

"For some reason, I think it will be fine." He leaned over and flicked the ratty rabbit's foot hanging from the key in the ignition. "Only one way to find out." He gestured for her to turn the key.

Momentarily derailed by the nearness of his big, hot body, it took her a beat to remember how. She turned the key, dimming the headlights as the engine struggled to spark to life. After a couple of loud, rattling attempts, Betty's engine roared.

"Good ol' Betty," she said and hit the gearshift into drive.

She drove slowly and carefully back to the old barn, constantly checking the rearview mirror for any signs of another fire sparked by the truck as they passed over the dry grass or the reignition of the one they'd just put out.

"It'll be okay," Liam said, his voice softened and reassuring. "We really soaked that grass up there. And I doubt the engine or muffler will get hot enough going such a short distance."

Appreciating his understanding, she nodded, but she couldn't fully relax until she'd backed Betty into her spot in the barn and shut her off.

Honey was still sitting exactly where she'd been told to stay.

As he climbed out of the truck Liam said, "Now that's a good dog."

"Right?"

"If you want to check your horses, I'll refill Betty's water tank." He didn't say *just in case the fire restarts*, but it was clear from his tone that was what he was thinking.

While she didn't doubt her ability to handle any crisis that might arise on her ranch when she was here alone, an ever-expanding gratitude for his help closed up her throat. She slid out of Betty and returned the key ring to its hook, giving the old rabbit's foot a thankful pat and a good scrubbing pet to her dog.

Before she left the barn with Honey at her heel, she cleared her throat and said, "If I'm not back before you're done, go ahead and make yourself at home in the house." Words she'd never thought she'd utter to this particular Neisson.

He paused in the act of dragging the barn's water hose toward the tank mounted in the pickup's bed. She noticed again how filthy he'd become fighting the fire. How hard he had worked to save her ranch. Appreciation for his efforts made her chest tight.

Or had he been working to save a ranch his grandfather might want to buy?

A different sort of tightness seized her chest and marred her gratitude toward him.

Liam stared at her, thinking heaven knew what, before giving a sharp nod. "Okay. Thanks."

This was the moment to say, no, thank *you*, but she couldn't do it. Not with so many doubts about his motivations, so she turned and practically ran with Honey to the horse barn. Her sanctuary.

Most of the twelve horses she'd stabled had returned from their individual paddocks to their stalls, settling down for the night. She wasn't the least surprised Whiskey Throttle wasn't one of them. The night air was still tinged with the scent of smoke, and instinct had him standing vigilant against the threat. It took a scoop of molasses rolled oats rattling in his feed bucket to lure him inside his stall so she could shut him in for the night along with the others.

She lingered in his stall, mucking it out and adding fresh straw. She finally stood, stroking his satiny cheek and strong neck, soothing herself as much as him. It had been a day.

Knowing she couldn't avoid facing the other strong, compelling male currently on her ranch indefinitely, she left the stable. The old barn door was closed and lights were blazing within the house, so Liam must have finished refilling the water tank and done as she'd suggested—made himself at home. In her home.

She refused to consider why the notion set her heart racing and made her palms sweaty.

Wiping her hands against her grubby jeans, she and Honey made their way to the side door of the ranch house. It didn't lead to a dedicated mudroom like they had at the Wright Ranch house, but did open to a laundry room of sorts. The washer and dryer were just inside the door, in the short hall that led from the side door to the kitchen. So she had a laundry hall, she supposed.

She'd be able to strip off her muddy, smoke-saturated clothes, toss them into the washer and dress in clean clothes from the dryer, the closest thing she had to a go-bag, before Liam even knew she was in the house.

Being as quiet as possible, she opened the side door and she and Honey stepped into the laundry hall. She eased the door closed while Honey busied herself drinking from one of her many water bowls stashed around the ranch. Amanda turned from the door and yanked her shirt over her head as she toed her boots off. The shirt went straight into the washer.

She pivoted toward the kitchen while she unfastened her pants, her attention on the closed dryer as she tried to remember if her favorite Henley and sweats were inside and came face-to-face with Liam holding an armful of clothes on his way to the washing machine.

Wearing nothing but one of her bath towels slung low on his lean hips.

The clothes bundled in his arms were the ones he'd had on, including the shirt he'd tossed into the corner of the truck bed.

She could only stare at him, struggling to keep her jaw from dropping. Liam was a big, strong man, but to see blatant evidence of that strength in the sculpted muscles of his arms, chest and—heaven help her—his six-pack abs robbed her of speech. It seemed her imagination hadn't been that far off the mark when she'd fantasized about him. She broke out in a full-on sweat.

His gaze seemed stuck on her chest, and the fact she was standing there in her bra hit her like she'd been shoved into a cold trough. Despite being well-covered by her serviceable and thankfully not ratty bra, she folded her arms in front of her.

After a couple of blinks Liam's gaze rose to hers. Maybe she was imagining things, but his eyes appeared a much darker blue.

He lifted one muscle-capped shoulder. "You said to make myself at home."

She had. And he had. Though she couldn't recall ever seeing him wandering around the Wright Ranch house in nothing more than a towel.

Honey abandoned her water dish to sniff at Liam's bare feet and shins. She gave the top of one foot a quick lick then wandered over to her dog bed in a corner of the living room.

Liam smiled bemusedly at the dog before looking back at Amanda. "I thought I'd get these"—he nodded toward the clothes in his arms—"into the wash before I jumped in the shower. On the off chance Drew's go-bag change of clothes aren't clean. Or in case he packed just basketball shorts and a tank top." His brows furrowed. "Which is actually more likely." He stared at her. "If that's okay."

Her brain finally reengaged. "Yes. Of course. To everything."

His blond brows twitched.

She reached back into the washer to retrieve her shirt but he stepped forward and dumped his clothes into the machine.

"No point in doing more than one batch of mud and smoke-covered clothes."

Her tongue seemed to be stuck to the roof of her mouth thanks to all the bare, heat-radiating male skin so close to her. What was wrong with her? This was Liam, her best friend's brother.

He smiled down at her, his gaze flicking briefly back down to her chest.

Who was she kidding? She knew exactly what was wrong with her. This was Liam, her best friend's brother.

Who she'd had a crush on for as long as she could remember.

★

LIAM HONESTLY HADN'T meant to surprise Amanda wearing nothing but a towel, but she'd been quicker than he'd expected her to be. He'd thought he could get his clothes into the wash and himself in and out of the shower before she returned. Because Amanda fussed over her horses as much as he did, he'd fully expected her to take as much time as necessary to calm her prized animals. Exactly what he would have done with his own horses. Thankfully, he could count on Mitch, his best wrangler, to care for the broncs while he was otherwise occupied.

He might not have intended to surprise her, but it seemed he couldn't work up any regret for his timing. Despite the fact he wouldn't be getting the sight of her in her little black bra out of his head any time soon. Coupled with the memory of her lips on his…

The shower he'd planned on taking was going to have to be a cold one now.

He cleared his throat. "I hope you don't mind I borrowed a towel."

"Not at all. I'm glad you did."

He wasn't sure if he laughed or coughed.

She skirted around him to get to the dryer. "I'll just get another one from here. Along with a shirt…"

While he wanted to tell her not to bother on his account, he also didn't want to make her uncomfortable. More than he already had by standing there wearing only a towel, that was.

So, he said, "I'll just hit the shower." Even though he'd be going back out to the burned patch of pasture and fence in a couple of hours—or sooner if need be—he wanted to wash off the worst of the soot and grime.

She pulled something from the dryer—a pillowcase, maybe—and straightened with it held against her chest. "Okay. Good. Uncle Red probably left his shampoo—"

"Shampoo?" Last he'd looked Red was pretty much bald.

She smiled for the first time today and it smacked him

right in the sternum. "He uses it on his beard."

"Ah. Gotcha."

"And I figured you wouldn't want to use mine. It's very fruity."

He nodded in agreement. Not because he had a problem with smelling fruity, but because he was having a hard enough time keeping her out of his head. Having her scent literally on him would be torture. "Thanks."

With one last glance, despite his best intentions, at what he could see of her bare shoulders and arms not covered by whatever she'd grabbed from the dryer to cover herself with, he turned and made his way back to the bathroom.

The old-style ranch house on the Sky High Ranch was actually smaller than the ranch manager's house where Ian lived over at the Wright Ranch, with only a kitchen, living area, two bedrooms, a single bath, and, of course, the little laundry area where Amanda had begun to strip. Liam thought it perfect. He'd spent his life feeling as though he lived in a high-end resort clubhouse. This place felt more like a home.

He'd already brought Drew's go-bag into the bathroom, and he unzipped the duffel to double-check there was indeed clothing of some kind packed inside. He found a pair of olive-green sweatpants, a black T-shirt and a black zipped hoody. Liam heaved a sigh of relief that he wouldn't have to hang around wearing nothing but a towel. Especially after getting an eyeful of Amanda without her shirt, her face smudged with soot and mud in a way that somehow made her even more attractive.

Yep, a cold shower was in order, and not simply to keep from using up all the hot water. He dropped the towel and stepped into the combined tub and shower, turning the cold tap on full to clean off his skin, cool his blood, and clear his mind.

His grandfather had sent him over here to do a job. He had been sent to Sky High to inspect and assess the condition of this ranch, to see if it met Thomas Wright's standards. And now that there had been a fire, he'd been charged with making sure the grass didn't reignite and that no further damage was done. Also, most importantly, to keep Amanda safe.

For himself, he needed to get a closer look at Amanda's new stallion.

These were the things he should be thinking about. The only things.

But even after a full ten minutes beneath the shower's cold spray all he could think about was getting another look at Amanda in her bra and discovering if her skin would feel as soft beneath his fingers as it looked.

CHAPTER SEVEN

Keeping an ear open for the sound of the shower shutting off, Amanda found a bath towel in the dryer and shucked off her remaining clothes, heavy and stiff with water and mud. The backsplash from the truck-mounted water tank hose had soaked her to the skin. After retrieving her phone from her jeans' pocket and setting it atop the dryer, she tossed her shirt, jeans, underwear and socks into the washing machine with Liam's clothes and wrapped the towel securely around her.

All with her hands shaking more than they had before her very first money-purse barrel race. She told herself she was quaking from cold, which was a plausible excuse. While the evening had successfully clung to the heat of the summer day, here on the high desert heat dissipated quickly as the night deepened. But the excuse was a flimsy one because she knew for a fact her temperature rose dramatically every time Liam was near. And having him in her house, naked, was definitely near enough.

Her bare toes curled on the glossy yellow tile that had been popular when her parents built this house as she put soap in the clothes washer. She paused with her hand on the knob. If she started the washer now, with Liam in the shower, there was a very good chance he'd be hit by a blast of cold water. She shrugged and started the load on a quick wash setting. When Red did it to her he claimed the cold water built character.

And she needed to get his clothes washed. The last thing she wanted was Liam hanging around in nothing more than a towel and a ridiculous amount of male sex appeal. She'd go up in flames for sure. Odds were good the happy-go-lucky Drew didn't actually have a change of clothes in his go-bag. Even if he did have extra clothes included in the duffel he'd given Liam, Amanda had serious doubts that anything of Drew's would actually fit Liam.

While Ian was the tallest of the Neisson boys, Liam was definitely the most muscular, with a breadth of shoulder and chest that—having just seen it up close in all his bare glory—she could safely say made him a much bigger man than his brothers. Especially his lankier younger brothers, Drew and Alec. Wrangling his bareback and saddle broncs himself had undoubtedly contributed to the drool-worthy dimensions of his physique.

Not wanting to come face-to-chest with his physique while she herself was wrapped only in a towel, Amanda scurried past the bathroom and into her bedroom. She closed the door with a quiet *click* then unwound the towel and tossed it on her bed. She fully intended to shower, also, but hanging out in her robe wasn't any more appealing than just a towel. Running on her bare toes to her dresser on the opposite wall, she yanked out the first bra, underwear, jeans, and shirt she encountered and dressed as quickly as she could. Which wasn't quickly at all with her cold, damp skin and shaking hands.

She'd just pulled on one sock when the bathroom door opened. While she'd told Liam to make himself at home earlier, the thought of him snooping around the inside of her house set her heart racing even more. Not because she had anything to hide—she lived with her uncle, after all—but she hadn't expected company of any sort, let alone him, when she'd left for the Wright Ranch earlier today.

She'd only been looking for a way out of the dark pit she'd slipped into when Red had handed her the letter from the noteholder's lawyer. Thomas Wright had indeed offered her a way out, but at what price?

Pride and a hearty dose of paranoia had her bolting for her bedroom door with the sock she had yet to put on gripped in her hand.

And came face-to-thankfully-clothed-chest with Liam. Drew had indeed come through for him with the go-bag, providing a black shirt, hoody, and green sweat pants for Liam to wear.

"Oof." Liam blew out as he caught her by her biceps to steady her. "We have to stop meeting like this, Amanda."

"Oh, geez, I'm sorry." She tried to step back and away from him, but he didn't let go of her.

He glanced down at her *Ride It Like You Stole It* graphic T-shirt, hastily donned jeans and lone sock. A small smile tugged at his mouth. "Why are you dressed?"

Having never imagined she'd hear those words from

Liam, she stammered, "Wh-why?"

"Aren't you going to shower?" As if to prove the need, he released her arms, licked the pad of his thumb and used it to rub at something on her cheek just like his father had.

If anyone else currently on this planet tried to scrub her clean like a parent would a toddler she would swat them away and tell them, as colorfully as she could, to keep their spit to themselves because she could wash her own damn face. But Douglas didn't count and it appeared Liam could touch her—spit or no spit—however he pleased. She swayed toward him instead of pulling away, tingles of sensation spreading from his thumb on her cheek all the way to the soles of her feet.

Struggling to focus, she said, "Umm, yeah. But my clothes were soaked, and I didn't want to subject you to me in nothing but a towel."

His thumb froze on her cheek. Something shifted in his gaze and he looked at her like he had before he'd kissed her earlier. Then his thumb began moving over her cheek again but his touch was lighter, definitely more of a caress.

When he spoke, his voice was low and rumbling, from deep in his broad chest. "Subject me? More like make my day."

She smiled, bemused. "Seeing you in just a towel nearly made me pass out."

"Oh, yeah?" His head slowly dipped toward her.

She instinctually rose up on her toes to further close the gap between them. "Yeah."

Nothing had changed since their first kiss before the fire.

He still wanted the stallion she'd staked her future on, the animal that could make her dream of being a top breeder of barrel racers come true. He still had the power to stop his grandfather from helping her pay off the promissory note with nothing but a negative word about the state of her ranch. And he was still, and always would be, her best friend's brother.

As before, none of it mattered. At least not right now, in this moment.

She reached up to grab hold of his black hoody to anchor herself, her other sock forgotten in her grip. As his lips grew near, his warm breath mingled with hers. Intoxicating. She tightened her fingers in the cotton hoody, the heat of his chest radiating through it and the black T-shirt beneath. He'd used her uncle's body wash and shampoo, but smelled nothing like Red when she filled her lungs with his clean, masculine scent.

Liam slipped his hand from her cheek into her hair, further anchoring her.

A blaring rendition of the song "Save a Horse, Ride a Cowboy" and the buzzing vibration of plastic on metal jarred Amanda out of the spell Liam had cast on her. She jerked back away from him. It was her phone, vibrating on the dryer where she'd left it. And she'd assigned that particular ringtone to only one person.

Caitlin.

Amanda lurched a full step back away from Liam as if Caitlin herself had walked in through the laundry hall.

Liam raised his brows. "Old Red?"

She forced a laugh in an attempt to cover for the intensity of her reaction. "Not with that ringtone. His is 'Good Ride Cowboy.'" She started inching toward the laundry space.

His brows dipped at her movement away from him. "Then who?"

Layers of guilt heated her face. "Caitlin."

"Ah." There was a wealth of understanding in that single word.

She turned and ran for her phone, her single bare foot slapping on the tile. Caitlin must have heard about the fire from one of her other family members. No way could Amanda leave Caitlin hanging to worry while Amanda made out with Liam.

Liam. Caitlin's brother. Her stomach flipped. What was she thinking?

Amanda skidded to a stop on her one sock in front of the dryer and snatched up her cell phone.

She hit the green answer button. "I'm here. Hey."

"Amanda! Are you okay? I just talked to Dad and he said your ranch was on fire. And Red's not there, right? Bodie and I are on our way."

Amanda was finally able to get a word in edgewise. "No! Don't come." She threw a panicked look toward Liam, who had wandered toward her, twirling her sock in one hand. When had she dropped that?

"The fire is out, Caitlin," he said loudly enough for his sister to hear him.

The heat of his breath still on her lips, Amanda silently

shushed him.

He rolled his eyes at her and, stuffing her sock into the pocket of the zipped-up hoody, went into the kitchen to hunt in the fridge.

"Was that Liam?" The shock was clear in Caitlin's voice.

"Yes. Yes, it was." Amanda turned away from the sight of Liam's well-formed backside as he bent to inspect the lower shelves of the refrigerator. Her brain threatened to turn off when presented with that view. "Your dad told him to stay here to make sure the fire doesn't reignite."

"Then it was bad. We're still coming." Caitlin could be heard giving instructions to Bodie to get dressed.

"No, Caitlin. Seriously. Everything is okay. The ranch wasn't on fire. It was just a little grass fire up by our gate. Your brothers, dad, grandfather, and the Wright Ranch hands came over with the water tanker and put it out." Amanda purposely glossed over the fact that Liam had already been here inspecting her ranch. She refused to burden Caitlin until Amanda knew more.

Nor would she tell her about the cigarette butts, for an even more compelling reason. Caitlin had almost been killed by a disgruntled former hand. Learning someone had been loitering between their properties would send Caitlin into a panic.

And as comforting having Caitlin here would be, Bodie Hadley and Liam Neisson in the same room would be about as pleasant as having a bear and a cougar sharing her couch. They were getting along better since the truth behind Bodie's bull-riding, career-ending wreck had come to light, but the fact that a cousin Liam had been close to had died in the same accident made the going rough.

Caitlin was silent for several beats. Amanda could picture her struggling with her need to protect those she cared for and what Amanda was telling her.

Finally, she said, "And Liam is going to stay there all night?"

Amanda let out the breath she'd been holding. She was making headway. "He is." Her heart gave a bump.

It would be so much easier to ignore the implications of Liam spending the night if she hadn't just been on the brink of kissing him. Again.

She straightened her spine and did her darnedest to sound nonchalant. "He's going to check on the burned area during the night to make sure the fire doesn't start up again. But I don't see how it could. We really soaked it. Plus, your grandfather's men and your brothers went at it hard with shovels."

Caitlin's sigh was loud through the phone. "Okay. Okay," she repeated herself, slowly and purposefully, as if working to convince herself. "And you're sure you, Honey, and your horses are all right?"

Amanda glanced at the dog in her bed, sprawled on her back and snoring, then turned back to face the kitchen. Liam was watching her as he ate a rolled-up piece of sandwich meat, one elbow propped on the eating bar top that separated the kitchen from the living area. She was inanely struck by the thought they hadn't stopped to eat anything the entire time Liam had been here. Food had been the last thing on her mind. And the way Liam was looking at her, as if he'd like to snack on her the same way he was the sandwich meat, made thinking of much else nearly impossible.

"Amanda?" Caitlin asked through the phone.

Giving herself a mental shake, Amanda said, "I'm fine. Honey's fine. The horses are fine. Everyone's fine."

A knowing smile teasing his mouth, Liam raised his meat snack in salute, clearly supporting her declaration.

Caitlin made a noise of reluctant acceptance. "If you're sure."

"I'm sure, Caitlin. But thank you." Amanda truly appreciated her best friend's concern.

"Are you still going to compete in your go-around tomorrow?"

Amanda put her free hand to her forehead. She'd forgotten about the barrel race she'd entered. And despite how tired she was, there was no way she'd back out of a competition. "Of course. Why wouldn't I?"

"Because your ranch was just on fire, that's why."

"A patch of grass—"

"Okay, okay. I'll try to make it to the rodeo grounds in time to watch you."

"Thanks, Cait." Amanda dropped her hand from her forehead and her gaze to her one sock-covered foot and one bare foot. She was thankful for Caitlin's friendship for too many reasons to count.

"I'm glad you're okay. I wouldn't be able to bear it if anything happened to you. And not just because you're my maid of honor. I love you. Try to get some rest."

Amanda's throat threatened to close. "I will. Night."

"Good night, Amanda."

Amanda had barely hit the red button to end the call when Liam's phone rang—no personalized ringtone for him—in the pocket of Drew's black hoody. He straightened away from the raised counter, finished off the meat roll as only a strapping man could and fished his phone out.

After a quick glance at the caller ID, he shot her a raised brow look as he answered the call. "Yes, Caitlin."

It sounded more like an answer to every question he knew she'd be asking him rather than a greeting. He winked, confirming Amanda's suspicion.

He listened to his sister as he chewed. "Yes. Yes." He listened some more. "I will. No, I do not need Bodie's help." He practically growled that, his expression changing from mildly amused to annoyed in a flash. He shifted his gaze away from Amanda as he listened to his sister. "Fine. I promise, Cait." His expression softened again.

An unexpected pang of longing pierced Amanda. She had Red and Caitlin, but to be a real part of a larger family was another fantasy of hers.

"Don't worry. I'll talk to you tomorrow. Bye." He ended the call.

Firmly squashing her ache to belong, she tried for a light tone. "She threatened you?"

"Of course. The old syrup in the boot routine." He didn't sound concerned. "But I am supposed to take care of you." He started toward her, looking an awful lot like the cougar she'd thought of earlier.

She took a step back. Not out of fear, but because she suddenly had the urge to find out what being eaten by a cougar would feel like.

He indicated the brown couch angled toward the stone fireplace and Uncle Red's ancient big-screen TV next to it. "Take a seat."

Normally, she would have told him to take a hike, but not today. Today had been a day of firsts that left her feeling exposed, vulnerable, and in need of a bit of care. She went to the couch and sat, watching him warily. A heady anticipation began to thread through her veins.

Liam moved to stand in front of her and squatted down onto his haunches. He met her gaze with those blue Neisson eyes of his, then looked down and tapped at the back of her right calf with his fingertips.

"What are you doing?"

"Lift your foot," he said, pulling her wayward sock from the hoody pocket.

He wanted her to raise her bare foot and had tapped at her leg to signal her like he would a horse that needed its hoof checked. Was he intending to put her sock on for her? The notion, coupled with the sight of his big body so low and near, sent a flush rushing through her. Out of self-defense she ignored what he was doing and instead focused on how he was doing it.

She leaned forward. "In case you haven't noticed, I am not one of your horses, Liam."

He looked up, a definite spark in his eyes. "Trust me, I noticed."

Whether it was the way he said it or the way he looked while saying it, she found herself popping her bare foot right up without a word.

"Thank you." He caught her leg behind her ankle and propped her heal on one of his muscular thighs. Gathering the length of the sock up on itself, he stretched it open and eased it on over her foot.

The feel of his knuckles skimming over the bare skin of her foot was the most erotic thing Amanda had ever experienced. Boy, did she need to date more. Or just throw caution to the wind and have her way with Liam.

Not. Going. To. Happen.

Best friend's brother.

Still she stared at him, her breath caught in her throat, as he finished pulling the blue striped sock all the way up and smoothing it in place.

Then he slapped her lightly on the opposite knee and said, "There you go. I promised Caitlin I'd take care of you." He straightened and stepped back, looking down at her. "What do you want to eat?"

Amanda mentally sputtered, trying to catch up. Had he just shifted from hot, kissable guy to… babysitter? Irritation swept away her momentary slip of sanity.

"I need to shower." She pushed to her now equally clothed feet and slipped past him. Furious at herself for daring to indulge herself in the fantasy that was Liam, she escaped to the bathroom without looking back.

And took a very cold shower.

WITH THE DETACHABLE floodlight from his ATV in hand, its broad beam dancing off the shin-high grass, Liam trudged up to the burned section of Amanda's pasture. Not because he was worried the fire had restarted. He honestly believed they'd smothered the area with enough water and dirt to prevent the grass from reigniting.

He was heading back to the fence line to look for more cigarette butts. Or any other sign that the fire had been set either purposefully or from carelessness.

Either way, whatever the intent, someone had been on Amanda's property when they shouldn't have been.

But for what purpose? Was Amanda in danger? Or had it been some transient who'd wandered way off the beaten path?

Liam had waited until he could hear Amanda in the shower before he'd left the house. He didn't want to worry her any more than she already was from the state of her ranch being in limbo. And he needed a hearty dose of fresh air to cool his jets. Apparently the cold shower he'd taken hadn't done the trick.

He'd almost kissed Amanda Rodrigues again. What was wrong with him? He needed to keep his distance from her so whatever recommendation he gave his grandfather regarding the condition of her ranch would be impartial. And the last thing he wanted was to be seen as using her to get to the stallion he wanted to buy from her. He wasn't that guy.

Or was he? The question bounced through his mind like

the beam of the floodlight bounced as he walked. To dispel the disquieting notion and distract himself, he raised the floodlight to illuminate the fence line he was heading toward.

A figure was crouched at the base of a singed fence post, on Amanda's property.

Adrenaline hit Liam's system and he stopped short. He was about to shout for the person to identify themselves when the figure looked toward him and stood.

Ian.

His oldest brother, wearing his dark brown cowboy hat, brown canvas barn jacket and dark washed jeans, waited silently for Liam to reach him.

When he did, Liam said, "Didn't Dad tell you I was staying here to keep an eye on the burn?"

"He did." Ian toed a glob of blackened grass and mud with his cowboy boot. "But I wanted to look some more for any sign of accelerant."

"I had the same thought."

Ian nodded, his expression thoughtful as he studied the ground at their feet. "Did Amanda say anything about who she thought could have been smoking up here?"

"No. Could the smoker have been a transient?"

"That's a possibility."

Liam looked down the fence line. "A long way from the road, though."

"It is," Ian agreed.

"Did Grandfather fill you in on why Amanda came over this morning?"

"He did." Ian tested the nearest fence post, which wobbled dramatically in the softened ground.

"Do you think the letter she received and the fact that someone was standing up here long enough to smoke three cigarettes are related?"

"Could be."

Liam's stomach muscles contracted at the thought. To what length would the mysterious noteholder go in order to obtain the ranch? But why a fire?

He put voice to the question. "But why start a fire on property whose ownership is about to be contested?" If the noteholder really wanted the ranch, then it wouldn't make sense to burn it. Liam didn't like when things didn't make sense. It pissed him off.

Ian shrugged. "To encourage Amanda to comply to avoid the additional expense of repairs and simply turn the deed over? I don't know." Ian kicked at the clump again. "Maybe whoever was standing here didn't realize a smoldering cigarette butt is enough to start a grass fire."

Liam scoffed. "At the end of a long, hot summer? Yeah, right. Plus, there were three butts which suggests someone stood there a while." Another thought intruded. "Or they'd deliberately set three lit cigarettes to burn in hopes that one or all would catch the grass on fire."

Ian buried his hands in his coat pockets, his expression grim. "Do me a favor?"

"What?"

"Keep close to Amanda. At least until Old Red gets back from Calgary."

No way in hell would Liam do otherwise. "Already promised Caitlin I would."

Ian nodded as if he should have known their sister would have already made the request. "Okay. Good. I'll be able to sleep knowing Amanda isn't by herself while we figure out what's going on here."

Ian might be able to sleep, but Liam sure as hell wouldn't. And not because of some mysterious chain-smoker. The memory of the feel of Amanda's lips beneath his would keep him awake just fine.

CHAPTER EIGHT

Amanda climbed from her cold shower, only slightly cooled down thanks to Liam's sock application, and hurried to dress again.

The cold shower had helped her wrist, though it was still tender to move. Not surprising after using it to pump water out of Red's truck-mounted tank. She reached for the athletic tape to rewrap it, then decided against it. No reason to give Liam continued reason to question her ability to handle her horse.

Even though it was late, she needed to call Uncle Red. If Caitlin had heard about the fire already, Red might get wind of it, also. Amanda didn't want him jumping to the wrong conclusion as Caitlin had, imagining their ranch reduced to a smoldering heap of ashes.

She'd still had her phone in her hand when she'd stormed into the bathroom, so to avoid the distraction that was Liam, she picked up her phone from the bathroom counter and called Uncle Red.

The phone rang several times before it was answered.

"Hello?" It wasn't Uncle Red, but a woman who'd answered.

Thinking she must have somehow hit the wrong name in her contacts list, Amanda looked at the screen of her phone. Nope, she'd dialed her uncle's number. Oh, man, what now?

She put the phone back to her ear. "Umm, I'm trying to reach Red Rodrigues?"

The woman said, "This is Red's phone. Who is this?"

"His niece, Amanda." Had the woman not looked at the caller ID? "Is my uncle okay?"

She heard a male voice speaking to the woman and rustling as if the phone was being handed off.

"Amanda?" Sure enough, the phone had been given to, or taken by, Uncle Red. "Darlin'? Is everything all right?"

"Who was that who answered the phone?"

"It was Gretchen. She's my—a friend of mine I'm visiting up here."

Good God, Uncle Red had a girlfriend. Amanda closed the lid on the commode and sank down onto it. It wasn't that she wasn't happy for Red. She was. He'd been stuck here with her for a very long time. He deserved to go off and be with someone. But why did she have to find out about it today of all days?

"Are you okay, Amanda? That big idiot didn't put you on your butt again, did he?"

Of course the image of Liam *putting her on her butt* popped into her head, even though she knew very well that wasn't what Uncle Red had meant. She leaned her elbow atop the bathroom counter and rubbed the space between her eyebrows. "No, Whiskey didn't buck me off again."

"Were you able to ride him?" The hope and excitement

in his voice tore at her.

"No. I didn't even try today."

There was a pause. "Did you find out any more about the note?"

It was Amanda's turn to hesitate. She didn't want to tell her uncle about Thomas Wright's proposition until she knew if their ranch was going to pass Liam's sniff test.

"Amanda?"

"I'm here. No, I didn't find out anything. I'm calling to tell you—before you hear about it from anyone else—that we had a little fire today—"

"A fire!" His rough voice cracked.

"No, it's okay, Uncle Red. Everything is okay." She spoke quickly. "The animals, everything. It was just a little grass fire up by the fence line, but the guys from the Wright Ranch came with their big water tanker truck and put it out. Completely. It's completely out. No damage to speak of. Just the fence. A little. No worries. I just wanted you to hear it from me, and not think it was worse than it actually was." She finally petered out.

"Amanda, are you okay?" He used the tone he always used when helping her up out of the dirt.

She smiled into the phone. "Yeah. It gave me a thrill for half a minute, but I'm fine now. One of the Neisson boys is going to check on the patch during the night in case there's a flare-up, so I'm not worried." No need to tell him which Neisson boy.

"Which one?"

She sighed. She should have known he'd want specifics.

"Liam. Liam is going to hang around over here tonight."

"Good, good. That boy could kick-stomp a three alarmer."

Amanda blinked at her uncle's backhanded compliment of Liam.

"How did the fire start? Lightning?"

"No. I don't know—we don't know for sure how it started. Yet." No need to tell him about the three cigarette butts, either.

"I can start home tomorrow—"

She jolted to her feet. The last thing she wanted was for him to have to leave from… whatever he was doing. "No. You don't have to leave early. We have some pretty great neighbors, so I'm fine."

Red heaved a sigh. "If you're certain…"

"I am, Uncle Red. You enjoy yourself and I'll see you in a few days."

"Okay, darlin'. Love you."

"Love you, too. Bye." Amanda ended the call and heaved a huge sigh of her own.

What a day.

★

"WAS THAT IAN up there with you?" Amanda asked, standing in the open doorway of the Sky High ranch house, clearly waiting for Liam's return. She was still wearing the same jeans and T-shirt she'd changed into earlier, though on her feet she now wore fleece-lined suede boots. The light from inside the house glinted off her long dark hair, hanging wet down her back.

Liam stepped up onto the porch and he could smell her as he drew near. Grapefruit and something else. Mint? A weird combination, but on her it made his mouth water.

He turned to look over his shoulder toward where he'd just come from. Other than the swath of stars that always covered the sky on moonless nights such as tonight, the landscape was shrouded in darkness beyond the ring of light from the house. But the gate in the fence line atop the slight rise would be visible from where they stood when lit by the floodlight he was holding.

Liam nodded, turning back to her. "Yeah. That was Ian."

"He came all the way back out here to check the field?"

"You know Ian." Liam shrugged.

His oldest brother was renowned for his need to keep an eye on everyone and everything. Which was fine, because he was good at it. As long as Ian left the running of the bronc program on the ranch to Liam, Ian could mother all he wanted.

She frowned up at the fence line. "Didn't he know you stayed to keep an eye on the burn?"

"He knew."

"But—"

"It's late, Amanda." Liam didn't want to have to hedge about what he and Ian had been discussing. He moved to the doorway, expecting her to give way.

She stood her ground.

He contemplated pushing past her, but the smell of her

fruity, shower-fresh self made his thumb itch to retrace the path it had taken earlier across her now clean cheek. He was going to have a sleepless night as it was. So, instead, he tried to reason with her.

He said gently, "If you are going to race tomorrow, you need to get some sleep."

Her gaze flicked to the darkened hillside one more time before she sighed and stepped backward into the house.

He followed her inside and shut the door.

"Right," she agreed. "You're right. And you'll have to head back over to the Wright Ranch to load up your broncs and get them to the rodeo grounds."

Normally, he wouldn't dream of allowing anyone else to be in charge of loading and transporting his horses, but he'd given his word to remain close to Amanda. "Nope. I'm going to stick close to you, at least until we know who was up there." He pointed a thumb toward the burned fence line. "I'll have Drew or one of the other guys help Mitch load the broncs up and bring them." He could always count on his brother, and of all his grandfather's ranch hands and wranglers, he trusted Mitch the most.

Amanda blinked at him. "You're going to stick *close* to me?"

He moved to set the floodlight on the counter. "Relatively. It makes sense since I'm here."

She stared at him for a moment, probably because his home was a mere fifteen-minute ATV ride away.

And because he didn't want her thinking about the chain-smoking trespasser, he pointed at the couch and said,

"Do you have an extra pillow and blanket?"

She visibly swallowed, and gestured vaguely at the short hall to the bedrooms. "You don't have to sleep on the couch—"

His eyebrows shot up.

"When you could use Uncle Red's bed," she quickly added.

As much as he admired the old guy, there was only one bed he'd consider sleeping in here, and it wasn't Red's. "Thanks, but this is good." He went to the couch and patted the backrest stuffing.

"If you say so." She turned, muttering, "You're going to hang off." She went to a narrow closet in the hall. She returned with a folded, plush, quilted blanket and a pillow in her arms.

He took them from her, grazing her bare forearms with his fingertips despite his best intentions.

Her pupils flared.

His entire body responded as if she'd declared *take me cowboy, I'm yours.*

She hadn't. Instead, Amanda stepped back as if he'd waved a hot brand at her. "Well, good night," she said, brisk and crisp, as if trying to cover for her skittishness.

"Good night," he said back with a nod, lowering the blanket and pillow in front of himself to cover his involuntary response to her. The action was entirely unnecessary because she turned and fled to her room without a second glance.

Yep, it was going to be a long night.

★

AMANDA SLIPPED INTO the shower again before dawn, and not only because she needed help clearing her head after a mostly sleepless night. She'd woken from what little sleep she'd managed to get drenched in sweat thanks to nightmares about her ranch and horses burning up in an uncontrollable fire. And dreams about her burning up in Liam's arms.

Though she still had her morning chores to do, vanity had her dressing quickly in her race day clothes—bedazzled jeans, pink western shirt and pink-accented boots—and easing out of the bathroom as quietly as she could in her boots. She hadn't heard any sound coming from the living room or kitchen. If Liam had somehow managed to fall asleep on the couch and was still sleeping, she didn't want to wake him. He'd worked hard manning the pump on Uncle Red's old truck's water tank and deserved the rest.

She crept out to the living room, avoiding the floorboards she knew creaked, stealing herself for the reality of the sight of Liam sleeping on her couch. The man was devastating enough awake. She imagined the sight of Liam asleep, vulnerable and unguarded, would weaken her knees. Pulling in a steadying breath, she peered over the back of the couch.

And found the blanket neatly folded with the pillow placed atop it, exactly how she'd handed it to him. She whirled to look at the kitchen, but he wasn't there. No way would she have missed him. She glanced around, but saw no sign of him. Had he changed his mind and gone back to the

Wright Ranch to accompany his broncs to the rodeo, after all? An annoying wave of disappointment sluiced over her.

She went out the front door and looked toward the old barn, where they'd left the ATVs parked the day before. His top-of-the-line four-wheeler was still parked next to her beat-up old one. Liam was still here.

Tension flew from her like a dried thistle in the wind.

She should have been relieved when she'd believed him gone, not the other way around.

Shoving aside the troubling revelation, she looked toward the horse barn. Was he using this opportunity to closely inspect Whiskey Throttle?

Well, he could look all he wanted. No amount of cajoling or manipulation by Liam would convince her to sell that horse.

The damning thought had barely formed when movement near the burned fence line caught her attention. Liam, with Honey at his side, was walking through the burned patch of grass next to the fence. At some point in the night he must have moved their clothes from the washing machine to the dryer and run it because he was wearing the jeans and shirt he'd had on yesterday, clean of the mud and soot he'd accumulated fighting the fire. With the cowboy hat on his head tilted downward, he walked slowly, kicking at clumps of blackened grass and testing fence posts.

Regret for thinking badly of him made her wince.

Of course. He was already up doing what he'd stayed here to do—keeping her and her ranch safe.

Guilt and embarrassment filled all the spaces the fled tension had occupied. He was doing what he'd said he would do. What he'd promised he'd do. He was keeping her safe, taking care of her.

And she was romanticizing the big, bad Liam Neisson.

Annoyed with herself, she turned and went back into the house to brew some coffee to fill a thermos.

Another thought occurred to her. If he'd moved the wet laundry into the dryer, then he must have taken out the clothes she'd just left in the dryer after they'd dried. Trying to remember exactly what she'd washed last, she went to the laundry hall, expecting a big pile of clothes atop the drier.

Nope. Liam had neatly folded everything, including the panties she'd washed last. He'd given the silky bits their own, very tidy little pile.

Her face flamed as she imagined him holding them up, shaking them out, then carefully folding them into the neat little squares she herself could never manage. His calluses probably caught on the delicate, satiny material.

The image was actually a little erotic. A tingling started low in her belly.

What was wrong with her?

She scooped up the neat piles of clean clothes and hurried with them back to her bedroom.

Heaven only knew how many times she'd have to think it before it came true, but she needed to get a grip on herself.

★

HAVING WALKED EVERY inch of the burned section of

pasture and fence line and assuring himself the fire was out for good, Liam was about to give in to his urge to go into the horse barn when he noticed the ranch house's front door standing open. Amanda must be up.

He'd been tormented throughout the night by the thought of her, in bed, only paces away from where he was attempting to sleep on the couch. Especially after he'd moved their laundry from the washing machine to the dryer, folding the clothes already in the dryer. Actually seeing her panties, touching them, had not been good for his peace of mind.

Getting up and dressed to check on the field had been an easy choice.

He made his way back down to the house, Honey bounding beside him. As soon as he reached the porch the smell of freshly brewed coffee hit him. His mouth watered. Coffee, the cowboy IV.

He couldn't get his muddy, soot-covered boots off fast enough. He found Amanda in the kitchen, pouring coffee from a carafe into a steel thermos set on the breakfast bar.

"Is there enough for a cup right now?"

She turned and picked up an already filled mug from the opposite counter.

Handing it to him, she smiled and said, "Good morning."

Clearly, she knew a thing or two about cowboys. The coffee in the mug was very hot, very black, and very strong.

He gratefully accepted the cup. "Morning."

She went back to filling the thermos and screwed the top

on. "Everything still good up by the fence?"

"Yep. Nothing a thousand gallons of water couldn't handle."

She paused, her hands and focused on the thermos. "Thank you, Liam. Thank you for everything." Her voice was thick with emotion.

He set down his mug, wanting nothing more than to round the counter and gather her into his arms. She'd showered again. Her damp hair curled around her heart-shaped face and the fresh citrusy scent of her shampoo mingled with the sharp aroma of the coffee.

He stayed right where he was. "You're welcome, Amanda."

"Okay, then." She blew out a breath and set the thermos away from her decisively. "I just need to get my morning chores done in the horse barn, then we can load up Rumbles and get to the rodeo grounds."

He eyed her getup with raised brows. "You intend to muck stalls dressed like that?"

She kicked out a hip and planted her fist on it. "Are you implying I can't shovel shit without getting it on me?"

He struggled to suppress a laugh. "Well, it is sort of an occupational hazard."

She walked past him toward the door with a flip of her dark curls over her shoulder. "I don't know how you do it, Neisson, but I shovel away from myself."

He chuckled and followed her. "Never doubted it for a second."

He downed the cup of bracing coffee, stomped back into

his boots, then trailed after her to the horse barn, damn near mesmerized by the play of early morning sunlight on her rhinestone-studded backside. God help him, she had a cute butt.

For his sanity's sake, he caught up with her then went ahead to pull open the stable door. The look she gave him dripped with suspicion, so he tipped his hat to her as she went by but refrained from *ma'am*-ing her. He had managed to learn a couple of things from having a sister like Caitlin. Like how not to annoy a woman early in the morning.

Between the two of them, they made quick work of turning the horses out into their paddocks, cleaning the stalls, feeding and watering each horse. Liam couldn't help lingering in Whiskey Throttle's stall after bringing in his flake of hay, which the horse immediately began pulling apart to eat. As the big red stallion set to devouring the section of the hay bale, Liam ran his hand over the animal's gleaming coat, feeling the well-formed muscles beneath.

Muscles made for bucking.

Out of the corner of his eye, he caught Amanda watching him from the stall door.

He turned toward her and held up his hands. "Just looking."

She scoffed and moved away.

With one last pat on Whiskey's flank, Liam left the stall to look for Amanda. He found her standing just outside the stable's main door staring up at the burned section of grass.

She said, "Normally, I'd turn the mares out in the back pasture and Whiskey in this pasture before leaving for the day." She left the *but* unsaid.

Liam knew what she meant. But... since there'd been a fire in the pasture, she was afraid to turn them out. An image of the cigarette butts on the burned ground came to mind. He'd be more afraid to keep them stabled.

"I think they'll be okay. Both Ian and I tested the fence post, and as long as Whiskey doesn't lean or rub hard on that section of fence it will hold."

She plucked at her cuff, obviously weighing her options.

"How's your wrist?" He didn't see any wrapping peeking from beneath her shirt cuff.

"It's fine." She rolled her wrist to give proof to her words, but the movement looked stiff and more than a little painful.

"Let me rewrap that."

She shook her head, covering the wrist with her other hand. "No, It's fine." She glanced at him. "But thanks anyway."

He let it go, deciding Amanda was synonymous with stubborn. He looked back to the burned section of pasture. "I could call Ian and have him send over a couple of hands to fix the fence and gate today." He left off *and watch over the place.*

Amanda met his gaze, her dark brown eyes swirling with turmoil. "Uncle Red will be back Tuesday."

"Did you call him and tell him about the fire?"

"Yeah. Last night after I'd showered. He wanted to come right home, of course, but I told him you were here..." She trailed off, leaving him to wonder if she was happy about it or not.

"And Red's okay with me being here?"

She nodded. "He basically said you were a good choice because you'd stomp the crap out of the fire if it restarted."

"He's not wrong."

Amanda rolled her eyes. "Anyway, he and I can handle the repair."

She was so damn independent. But she needed to be smart about this, too.

He waved a hand at the sea of grass, bleached pale yellow by the late summer sun. "At least let me have some of my broncs driven over here to graze down some of this excess grass fuel." And discourage any strangers from standing around, chain-smoking cigarettes.

"Sky High isn't part of the Wright Ranch yet, Liam." She spun on her boot heel and stomped back into the stable. From inside she yelled, "Just open the stable's pasture gate and the back pasture gate, please."

He did as he was told without comment, trotting through the stable to the other set of doors which he pushed open. He couldn't imagine how difficult having her home threatened, in multiple ways, was for her.

Liam had just swung the back pasture gate wide when the first of her mares came trotting out of the stable on her own, heading straight for the pasture gate he was holding open. The rest soon followed. There was no doubt they knew the routine. As soon as they cleared the gate the mares broke into a full out gallop, like the champion barrel racers they were.

He went to the lower gate near the stable that they'd driven the ATVs and the water truck through the day before and opened it. Amanda reemerged from the stable leading Whiskey Throttle and Rumbles. She dropped Rumbles's lead line and the mare stopped immediately, being well-trained to a ground tie. Whiskey danced to the side as she led him to the gate, his excitement over being turned loose in an open field obvious. She worked to unclip the lead from his halter, having to time her efforts with the tossing of his head.

As soon as the click of the lead line coming free of the halter's chin O-ring sounded, Whiskey Throttle was gone, galloping through the gate with his tail held high.

Liam closed and latched the gate. "You sure have a good eye for horseflesh, Amanda."

"Uncle Red was the one who found him and bought him."

"But you know what you have in him."

Her attention on her stallion, she didn't respond, but a small smile played at the edges of her pretty mouth.

"And you can one hundred percent shovel shit without getting any on you."

She smiled outright.

Inordinately pleased with himself for making her smile, he followed her as she led Rumbles to the side of the old barn where she'd parked the horse trailer hitched to her tan, club cab dually truck.

"Do you need any tack from the stable?" he asked as she loaded Rumbles into the trailer. Lugging a saddle would not do her wrist any favors.

"No, but thanks. I left my barrel saddle and everything else in the trailer's tack compartment after we were practicing the other day."

The day she caught his escaped bronc and received the letter that sent her to his grandfather. A good day and a bad day all in one.

She stepped down from the trailer and closed and latched the gate. "If you'll close up the barn, I'll heat us up a couple of breakfast sandwiches to eat on the way."

"If I'd known you had breakfast sandwiches I wouldn't have eaten all your deli meat."

Her laughter trailed after her as she headed toward the house.

He stayed where he was, watching the delectable sway of her sparkly backside and the bounce of her dark curls down her back, until she disappeared into the house. Then he gave himself a shake and hustled to close up the horse barn. He'd just finished when she came out of the house with the silver thermos in one hand and napkin-wrapped sandwiches in her other.

Making him coffee was one thing, but a breakfast sandwich? He could imagine Amanda all sorts of ways—mostly naked, lately—but acting all domestic? Not in a million years. He was grinning when she met him at the truck.

Her dark, winged brows dropped and she radiated suspicion as her gaze traveled over his face. "What?"

Count on Amanda to just come right out and ask. Another thing he really liked about her.

"I'd be a fool not to be happy about being served my

breakfast by a pretty lady."

She harrumphed and handed him one of the sandwiches, its warmth seeping through the paper napkin. She continued past him to her truck, placing the thermos inside the cab, then pulling a set of keys from her pocket. She climbed behind the wheel.

Not minding riding shotgun instead of driving, he climbed into the front passenger seat. While his mind should have been on the fire, the smoker, and the job his broncs needed to do during the rodeo today, the only thing he could think about on the way to the High Desert Rodeo grounds was the beautiful, spunky lady next to him.

CHAPTER NINE

When they arrived at the High Desert Rodeo grounds and the competitors' parking area in the back, Amanda pulled her dually and trailer next to the large, black horse trailer and matching truck custom painted with the Wright Ranch logo and parked. Her hands had grown sweaty on the wheel with Liam seated next to her in the truck. She was just so aware of him. It was more than a little nerve-racking.

Liam's men had already unloaded his bucking horses into the rough stock corrals. Amanda spotted several she recognized milling about the corral in front of where she'd parked. Including Wild Bill.

She turned to Liam seated in the passenger seat. His attention was on the horses in the corral also, his sharp gaze seemingly noticing everything.

"You think Wild Bill is ready to compete?" she asked.

"No. But I had Mitch load him up, anyway. The gelding still needs to get used to the sights and sounds of the rodeo."

"Yeah, he was a little on the feisty side the other day, wasn't he?" She grinned, unable to resist teasing him a little.

"Feisty is good, but only at the appropriate time." He

looked toward her with a smile, obviously remembering Wild Bill's unscheduled break from the bucking chute into the arena.

Then his gaze dipped to the opened buttons at the top of her western shirt and she imagined a different sort of feistiness.

She swallowed and forced herself back on track. "You'll get him there. If anyone can, it's you."

His expression sobered. "Thank you, Amanda."

She'd intended the comment to be offhanded, but her compliment meant something to him. Did he not know how good he was with his bucking horses? If anyone could handle a difficult horse, it was Liam. While he'd been quick to anger since he'd witnessed his mother being injured, he was never angry around the horses. Never. They had always appeared to be his balm.

Even if she was inclined, Amanda was prevented from asking Liam the question straight out because he quickly climbed out of the truck. He surprised her again by going to the back of her horse trailer rather than straight to the corral to check his horses. By the time she'd climbed out of the truck and went to join him at the rear, he already had the gate open and was backing Rumbles out of the trailer.

His touch was gentle and his tone encouraging. Like she'd just been thinking, he was good with horses. Something shifted in her chest.

Before she could process what she was feeling, Liam handed Rumbles's lead to her and moved to the trailer tack room at the front. He pulled her barrel racing saddle and pad and Rumbles's bridle from the racks.

"Liam, I can do that." She did it every single day, actually.

"I know." He handed her the bridle and settled the pad and saddle on Rumbles's back, not missing a beat.

Amanda rolled her eyes and slid the bit into her mare's mouth and the bridle onto her head.

As he fastened the girth strap and she secured the bridle cheek strap, she said, "You don't have to help me here, you know."

"I promised Caitlin." He glanced at her, his gaze almost tender.

"Dang straight you did," Caitlin said from behind Amanda.

Amanda turned to find Liam's lone sister striding toward them. Her blue eyes sharp and assessing, she was dressed in jeans, boots, a tan barn jacket and had left her long blonde hair loose beneath a black cowboy hat. Bodie Hadley followed in her wake, looking very much like the contented fiancé. And very much the former successful bull rider, all lean strength and easy confidence in his jeans, boots, striped long-sleeve shirt and brown cowboy hat.

Caitlin opened her arms and Amanda dropped Rumbles's reins to meet her halfway, accepting the comfort that could only come from a best friend's hug.

Caitlin whispered in Amanda's ear, "Are you okay?"

"Totally. It was just a little grass fire." Amanda quickly reassured Caitlin, but she couldn't quite make herself step out of the hug.

Caitlin gave her another squeeze. Caitlin knew her so well.

Getting herself together, Amanda extracted herself. "The cavalry came to my rescue, so it didn't turn into more."

Caitlin's gaze jumped over Amanda's shoulder to her brother and her blonde brows twitched upward.

Amanda turned to look at Liam also. He shrugged and gave one last tug on the girth strap before threading it back in on itself.

Bodie snorted. "What'd he do? Pee on it?" As a man who'd been gored by a bull he'd just rode, it took a lot to impress Bodie Hadley.

Liam lowered the stirrup and rested an elbow on the saddle seat. "At least I'm man enough to do it."

Caitlin said, "Oh, please. What is it with you two and your endless pissing contest?"

Amanda choked on a laugh. But what did Caitlin expect? She was marrying into a family her brothers had been trained since birth to hate.

Caitlin stepped closer to her brother. "And what's this I hear about cigarette butts? Did someone start the fire on purpose?"

Liam's gaze flicked to Amanda before returning to his sister's. So much for not worrying Caitlin before her engagement party. "Drew?"

Caitlin planted her fists on her hips. "Of course, Drew. Thank goodness I have at least one brother I can count on to let me know what is happening to the people I love."

It was Liam's turn to roll his eyes.

"Well?" Caitlin wasn't going to relent.

Amanda opened her mouth to tell Caitlin and Bodie what little they knew but Liam said, "It could have been intentional, but it was more likely accidental."

Bodie nodded. "There are a hell of a lot more reliable ways to set dry grass on fire if that's your intent."

Liam pointed at Bodie and nodded in a *what he said* way.

Caitlin wasn't placated. "But there was still someone standing on Amanda's property, carelessly smoking a pack of cigarettes."

"Three," Liam corrected. "Just three cigarettes."

Caitlin waved him off. "Whatever. Doesn't make it any less creepy." She turned to Amanda. "I'm worried."

Exactly what Amanda hadn't wanted. "Please don't be. I'm sure it was nothing." She assured Caitlin, even though she also thought someone standing above her ranch, smoking, was beyond creepy. It was terrifying.

"What about the promissory note? Why didn't you call me, Amanda?" Caitlin's bright blue eyes grew brighter with the sheen of tears.

Caitlin's pain turned Amanda inside out. "Because it will be fine. You don't have to worry. I'll figure it out."

Bodie stepped forward and slipped an arm around Caitlin. "But now everyone knows everything there is to know, and I'm sure *we'll* find a solution."

Amanda didn't miss his emphasis on *we'll*. But his reassurance clearly comforted Caitlin, who softened against him.

Instinctively, Amanda glanced at Liam and found him watching her instead of his sister and Bodie. Unlike Caitlin's eyes, Liam's blue gaze was inscrutable. Would he ever be the type of guy to quickly offer support like Bodie? And how would she ever resist him if he did?

He broke the spell with a tug on the saddle horn and a pat on Rumbles's shoulder. "Now that that's settled, Amanda has her first race to run."

Liam was right. She pulled in a centering breath and reclaimed Rumbles's reins. The normally spunky mare had fallen asleep, not the slightest bit interested in what the people were going on about. Amanda would have to wake her up.

Amanda stepped toward Liam to mount, but he didn't move out of the way.

He stared into her eyes with an intensity that had Amanda's heart pounding as if she'd been given a good run to wake up.

"You've got this," he said softly.

His confidence in her made her want to melt into him the way Caitlin did with Bodie. If that wasn't a reason to take off on her fastest horse, she didn't know what was. She had to stay strong on her own, as always.

He put his hands on her waist and for a horrifying second she thought he'd read her mind. But instead of holding her in place he picked her up as if she weighed nothing and set her on Rumbles.

Bodie stepped forward and handed her the reins she hadn't realized she'd dropped. "Go get 'em, tiger."

Caitlin held up her hands. "Wait. Where's your hat?"

Amanda slapped a hand over her bare head. Had she forgotten her hat? She couldn't compete without it.

Liam said, "It's in the truck."

Caitlin hurried to Amanda's dually and fetched the cream cowboy hat from the rear seat where Amanda had unwittingly left it. She came back and started to hand it up to Amanda, but Liam intercepted it.

He crooked his finger to get her to lean down toward him. He was tall enough she didn't have to lean far before she was close enough for him to settle the hat on her head.

She met his gaze. She'd had no idea blue eyes could hold such heat. Which transferred straight to her core when he pushed her hair behind an ear, knocking her hat askew.

Bodie cleared his throat. "You're going to make her miss her slot, Neisson."

Amanda bolted upright in the saddle, the path Liam's fingers had taken tingling. Caitlin was watching them with suspicion while Bodie looked vaguely disgusted.

Liam placed a hand on her thigh, regaining her attention. "Go fast."

The only way to go. Amanda gave him a sharp nod, straightened her hat, lifted her reins and shifted her weight forward to signal Rumbles it was time to move.

If only getting rid of the sensation of Liam's big, hot hand on her thigh like he was staking his claim was as easy.

★

LIAM POSITIVELY ITCHED with the need to go watch Amanda race, telling himself that his promise to Caitlin as well as

Ian's request required him to keep eyes on Amanda at all times. Deep down, it was because he was developing a raging need to keep other parts on her, also. He damn near burned to repeat the kiss they'd shared.

Instead of climbing to the platform above the chutes to watch the barrel racing heats, he forced himself to stay with his broncs, helping Mitch and his other bucking horse wrangler, Jon, double-check the horses for soundness before they were called on to buck during the saddle bronc and bareback competition later in the afternoon. But Liam's mind was definitely in the arena.

Amanda's name being announced on the PA froze his hand on the front fetlock joint of Karen From Finance, a big Clydesdale mix mare who was one of his best buckers. And she didn't like her feathery ankles messed with.

It was too early in the day for there to be much of a crowd in the arena stands, but those who were present cheered loudly enough for him to know Amanda and Rumbles had triggered the electric eye timer with her explosive entry into the arena. He stayed frozen, his breath trapped in his lungs, as he listened.

In his mind's eye, he saw her and her fleet buckskin quarter horse charging toward the first fifty-five-gallon barrel, Amanda's long dark brunette hair streaming behind her beneath her cowboy hat. She'd be encouraging Rumbles to gallop as fast as she could, then hanging onto the saddle horn as Rumbles curved around the first barrel. Rumbles would stay level heading toward the second barrel in the clover leaf pattern, then lean hard—

The crowd groaned.

The announcer said, "And the second barrel goes over like a tall man with small feet. That's a five second penalty, folks. Tough luck for our own Miss Amanda."

Liam jerked upright. A five second penalty was a death blow in a sport won by one-hundredth of a second. Amanda would be devastated.

But mostly pissed off.

As if concurring, Karen From Finance brought her chestnut head around and bit him on the elbow.

"Hey, knock it off," Liam told the horse.

Mitch, testing the hock on a big black gelding with white socks right next to him, chuckled. "You know Karen doesn't like those thick ankles of hers messed with. Especially when you're thinking about another gal."

Liam sent Mitch a glare, but the man was right. Distraction and rodeo rough stock did not go well together.

Mitch said, "I've got this if you want to go check on her." He hitched his head toward the arena so there would be no doubt which *her* he was referring to.

Liam hesitated. Caitlin and Bodie were probably there for Amanda, but maybe not. While Bodie wasn't contracted to provide any of his bulls for this rodeo, his family had supplied steers and calves for the various roping competitions and he and Caitlin could easily be helping them out rather than watching Amanda race. Which made Liam's decision to leave Mitch in charge yet again much easier.

"Thanks, Mitch. I won't be long."

"Not a problem, Liam. Go."

Liam tipped his hat at the long-time ranch hand and patted Karen as he walked around her to reassure her into not kicking him. Though nothing with these animals was guaranteed.

Just as it wasn't guaranteed Amanda would want to talk to him now. Didn't matter because he was going to check on her, anyway.

★

Amanda rode Rumbles straight back to her trailer after exiting the arena. Normally, she would have lingered to watch the other racers, cheering them on despite being in direct competition with them for rankings as well as prize money. This was rodeo, after all.

But not today.

The purse at this small rodeo wasn't much, and certainly not enough to help pay off the note on her ranch, but the amount wasn't of importance. With so many new and up-and-coming racers on the hunt for better barrel racing horses at these smaller regional rodeos, what mattered was her and Rumbles's performance. Who would want to buy a horse she'd bred or hire her to train their horses if she couldn't keep from reining her own horse into a barrel in the first go around?

Her head just hadn't been in the race. End of story.

She reined Rumbles to a stop next to her trailer and dismounted. She immediately flipped her stirrup over the saddle and started loosening the girth strap.

"Well, that sucked."

Amanda had to smile at Caitlin's concise assessment of her race. "That it did."

Taking hold of Rumbles's bridle, Caitlin started unbuckling the cheek strap. "I can't remember the last time I saw you drive into a barrel."

"It's definitely something I prefer to forget." Amanda slid the saddle and pad off her horse, who hadn't even broken a sweat. Her wrist tweaked her from the weight of the saddle. Okay, so maybe having Liam's help wasn't that bad.

"Don't beat yourself up, Amanda. You were fighting to keep your ranch from going up in flames last night." Caitlin turned and opened the door to the horse trailer's tack room for Amanda.

Amanda laughed at her best friend's sense of drama and stepped up into the tack room. "Like I said before, Caitlin, the fire wasn't that bad. It just burned a patch of grass and singed our gate." She hoisted the saddle and its pad onto the wire rack.

Caitlin's eyes went wide and paused handing Rumbles's bridle to Amanda. "It burned our gate?"

"Singed." Amanda took the bridle and hung it and the reins from its designated hook, then grabbed a trailer tie rope. "The fire singed the gate. And a couple sections of fence. Nothing catastrophic."

Caitlin harrumphed and moved to the side so Amanda could step down. "Still, you can't expect to run the best race of your life after something like that."

Amanda bit the inside of her cheek to keep from blurting

the reason she'd reined Rumbles into the barrel had more to do with Caitlin's brother Liam's touch, his presence in her house the night before, and—heaven help her—his kiss, than a measly grass fire.

Unless the fire had been intentionally set.

A chill chased over Amanda's skin as she clipped the one end of the tie-down to Rumbles's halter.

Caitlin grabbed a curry comb from a bin in the tack room and began grooming Rumbles's coat where the saddle had rested. "I take it you're done for the day here?"

Fighting an overwhelming sense of defeat, Amanda smoothed a hand over Rumbles's velvety nose. "Yeah. No way will I make it into the final round with a five second penalty. And I have plenty to do at home." The image of the burnt cigarette butts appeared in her mind. She shouldn't have left in the first place.

"Well, that sucked," Liam said behind Amanda.

She turned to see him sauntering toward them. His handsome mouth was kicked up in a wry smile, but his gaze was full of concern.

Amanda's heart thumped, heavy and ominous.

Caitlin laughed. "Way to be unoriginal, Liam."

His blond brows dipped.

"Your sister said the exact same thing," Amanda enlightened him.

"Were you watching?" Caitlin asked, an undeniably suspicious tone to her voice.

Liam shook his head, his gaze never leaving Amanda. "No, but I could hear the PA."

Caitlin asked, "Were you with the broncs?"

"Yeah."

"Looks like you were paying more attention to the PA than the horse closest to you." Caitlin pointed at the sleeve of his shirt where dirty halfmoons the precise shape of a horse's mouth encircled his elbow.

Amanda gasped and reached for his arm but stopped, hesitant to touch him if he was already hurt. "Oh, my gosh, Liam. Are you okay?"

He glanced down at his elbow as if surprised, then used his other hand to inspect the damage to his shirt. He sighed. "That would be a gift from Karen From Finance. And, yes, I wasn't paying attention to her."

Because he'd been paying attention to what was happening to Amanda in the arena. Amanda blinked at him. She couldn't remember anything distracting Liam from his horses before.

He shrugged and focused again on Amanda. "So what happened? Did she cut too close?"

"It wasn't Rumbles. She didn't do a single thing wrong." Amanda smoothed her hand down her mare's silky face, soothing herself more than the horse. "It was all me. I reined her smack into the second barrel."

Liam made the noise the Neissons made in their throats when whatever they might want to have said would not be polite and shifted his gaze to Rumbles's front shoulder. Amanda had to step out of his way as he moved to put his hands on the mare, clearly checking for injury.

The heat of shame filled Amanda's cheeks. She should

have checked Rumbles the second they'd ended their go. But she'd been too busy attending her own pity party.

Caitlin peered over her brother's shoulder. "I saw it happen. She didn't hit the barrel hard or catch an edge or anything. They just bumped it enough to knock it over."

As much as she appreciated Caitlin's defense of her, Amanda cared far more about her horse's welfare. And the truth was the truth. "I steered her right into it instead of around it. Is she okay?" Amanda trusted Liam to know.

While he wasn't a veterinarian, he had a degree in animal science from the state university's local branch that more than qualified him to care for and breed livestock. And he'd made caring for the Wright Ranch's bucking horses his whole life.

He ran his hands over Rumbles's chest, both her shoulders and both legs before standing and giving the patient horse a pat. "She's fine. It probably seemed worse to you because you've grown used to going around the barrels instead of through them."

"Told you," Caitlin quipped.

Amanda was still glad she'd already decided to pack it in for the day.

Liam's gaze traveled over Rumbles's back, clearly noting the lack of the saddle he'd put on himself. "You heading home?"

She nodded. "It's probably for the best."

Liam considered her for a moment, then looked to his sister who was staring intently at him. "Just give me a couple hours, then I'll come over and get to work on that fence."

Amanda wasn't sure if he was talking to her or Caitlin, but she said, "Uncle Red will fix it when he gets home next week."

Liam said, "That fence is as much our responsibility as it is yours."

Caitlin interjected, "Let him do it, Amanda. I'll feel better with him hanging around your place, anyhow."

The memory of Liam strolling toward her in nothing but a towel and a smile made Amanda's face heat again. That wasn't what Caitlin meant, but Amanda couldn't seem to form an argument against Liam's help.

She glanced at Liam. He was watching her in that predatory way of his. A big, dominant lion on the hunt.

But for what?

CHAPTER TEN

Feeling very much like a dog skulking home with its tail between its legs, Amanda drove her truck and trailer up the drive to Sky High Ranch. And the fact that she had the overwhelming need to scan as much of the fence line and pasture land that she could see made the sensation of defeat that much worse.

Thankfully, there was no sign of any lurking chain-smoker.

The thought of someone she didn't know on her property, or even on the Wright Ranch, gave her the chills. She checked the clock on the dashboard, mentally calculating how long until Liam would return. As much as her independent self might rebel against being babysat, having Liam at least within sight went a long way to settling her jangling nerves. She trusted him to protect her. The knowledge was sobering.

Out of habit, Amanda slowed as she passed the house, something she usually had to do to keep from hitting Honey when the dog charged out from her place on the porch to greet her, then remembered she'd put Honey in the house before she left. The horses would easily run away from people who didn't belong on the ranch, but Honey would run to greet them. A watchdog she was not. There was no such thing as a stranger to a golden retriever.

Amanda pulled up to the old barn and backed the truck and trailer into their spot next to the barn and parked. In the winter, when they could easily get several feet of snow, she'd make room for both in the barn. She used them too much rodeoing in the spring and summer to bother.

Amanda hurried from the truck, not wanting to make Rumbles stand in the trailer any longer than necessary. Not because the horse minded being trailered, she didn't, but guilt still tweaked Amanda for not thinking of Rumbles's well-being as quickly as Liam had. She unloaded Rumbles and led her toward the stable, intending to make amends with the horse by treating her to an extra serving of maple rolled oats.

The mares she and Liam had turned out into the back pasture were either standing at the fence, having seen her return, or grazing nearby. Normally, she returned much later when she'd been at a competition, and the horses left behind were accustomed to being fed as soon as she came home. Not today. They'd have to wait.

She expected Whiskey Throttle to also be at the gate to the pasture she'd put him in—it hadn't taken him long to learn the routine here at Sky High. But surprise washed over her when the horse wasn't there. She scanned as much as she could see of the pasture, but the stable blocked a sizeable portion of it. He must be grazing in the area behind the stable and hadn't noticed the truck and trailer returning. He was probably simply happy to be in an open field rather than his paddock or stall.

She should take advantage of this unexpected free time and work with him. She wasn't foolish enough to attempt to ride him again with Uncle Red gone. Nothing was worse than having to drive oneself to the hospital with a broken arm, or worse. But she could at least work Whiskey on the lunge line in the corral. Not only would it burn off some of the stallion's excess energy, but a session on the end of the long lead would help build the rapport between them. Something she desperately needed if she was ever going to stop his bucking.

If she could stop it.

Liam believed Whiskey had been born to buck.

Maybe Amanda had been born to prove him wrong.

Feeling reinvigorated with a challenge before her that she could actually have some control over, Amanda led Rumbles into the stable and to her stall. She gave the sweet mare a big scoop of grain and a quick rubdown. At the moment, Rumbles was the best advertisement Amanda had for the barrel racing breeding and training business she wanted to build, and she needed to take care of her. Plus, she flat out loved the silly animal.

With Rumbles settled, Amanda snagged the sturdy lead rope she used with the stallion as well as the long lunge line and training whip. She went back out of the stable to look for Whiskey. She would bring him down to the corral, then go to the house and change out of her racing duds. And let out Honey, who was undoubtedly having a fit by now over being stuck in the house.

Amanda didn't want to have to chase Whiskey in her good boots, so she went to the corral first and propped the whip against a post and draped the coil of lunge line over the same post. Whiskey didn't seem to mind working on his gates and balance at the end of the long rope, but he wouldn't want to leave the pasture if he knew that was what he'd be doing.

Pulling her hat lower to shade against the sun, Amanda turned and searched the pasture for her newest, most valuable horse. The entire pasture, clearly visible from where she stood, was empty. It took a beat and another visual search of the pasture for her brain to process what she was, or rather wasn't, seeing.

Whiskey Throttle was gone.

Amanda's lungs seemed to shrivel in her chest, reducing her to shallow, rapid breaths. Her vision narrowed and her heart beat so fast she feared it would burst from her chest.

No, she couldn't panic, not right now. She had to think. The one thing she feared she was incapable of at the moment.

She needed someone who could.

Amanda spun on her heel and ran for the house, Honey's barking from inside spurring her on. She hit the door with her shoulder the same instant she turned the knob, a trick for opening a door quickly that she'd perfected as a kid who'd taken the barrel racer's motto of *go fast* to heart.

She bounced off, the knob unyielding.

Locked. She'd taken the unusual step of actually locking

her doors before she and Liam had left this morning. Damn chain-smoker.

What if whoever had been up there, smoking, had been watching Whiskey Throttle? Planning on stealing her horse?

Her panic increased as she went up on her toes to find the key she and Red kept above the door, out of sight but easily accessible to those tall enough. Because who wanted to carry keys when out horseback riding?

She snagged the key with her fingertips and unlocked the door as quickly as she could with shaking hands. The moment she opened the door Honey burst out, pausing only long enough to bump Amanda with her nose before racing toward the dually. Probably looking for Liam.

Liam. He'd know what to do.

The sight of the truck and trailer reminded Amanda that she'd left her cell phone, with Liam's number newly programed into it, in the cup holder. Not bothering to shut the front door, Amanda took off for the truck, her boot heels thundering on the wooden porch. Having failed to find whatever she'd been looking for around the truck and trailer, Honey raced to join Amanda and ran with her back to the truck.

When she reached it, Amanda yanked open the passenger door and dove in to grab her phone. Draped across the seat with her legs hanging out of the truck, she found Liam's number and called it. His phone rang for what seemed a million times before Liam finally answered.

"Hello?" His tone was brisk, gruff. As if she'd interrupted something. She'd feel bad after she had her horse back.

"Liam? It's Amanda. Whiskey Throttle is gone and I don't know what to do. What if the smoker came back and took him? How will I—"

"Amanda, slow down. Are you okay? Are you hurt?"

His concern, so real and tangible, even over a cell phone connection, snapped her out of her panic. Her lungs expanded and she was able to breathe.

"No, I'm not hurt. I'm okay. As okay as I can be with my prized stallion missing."

"Was he gone when you got back?"

"Yes. At least I think so. I didn't notice right off, but I haven't been back long."

"Are any of the other horses missing?"

"No," she replied automatically, but realized she wasn't sure. She hadn't exactly counted when she'd looked toward them earlier. "But wait, let me check." She pushed herself upright and backed out of the truck. Walking forward so she could see around the nose of the dually, her heart rate increased at the prospect of discovering any more of her horses gone.

They were all there. Heads up and watching her as if they sensed something was wrong. Even Rumbles was standing in her paddock, head high and ears pricked toward her.

She blew out a huge breath. "No. The mares are all here."

"Could Red have come home and—"

"No." She cut Liam off, pacing back toward the truck. "When he found out you all had helped me with the fire he said he was staying at the rodeo he's working in Calgary. He's an event judge and can't just leave. And he would have called me if he'd changed his mind."

"Okay. Now, listen to me, Amanda. I need you to go back into the house and lock the doors. Keep Honey with you. I'm on my way."

He ended the call before she could respond. She looked at her phone and huffed at it. She wasn't some spineless female incapable of defending herself. Of its own volition her gaze went to the blackened swath of grass in the pasture Whiskey had been in. A person who would flick burning cigarettes into tinder-dry grass didn't have a shit bucket of concern for anyone or anything downwind.

Fine. She would lock herself in her own home. But she'd be damned if she'd cower.

★

LIAM'S HEART POUNDED in a way it had only done one other time. He broke into a run to reach his truck as quickly as possible. Thank goodness he'd had Jon follow Mitch and the broncs in it to the rodeo grounds.

His grandfather had taught them it was always a good idea to take more than one Wright Ranch vehicle to any given rodeo. Mostly so that if the truck pulling the rough stock broke down the animals wouldn't be stuck on the side of the road along with the truck, leaving a rodeo without the broncs, steers or calves it needed to be staged.

In his experience, he'd found the extra truck was most

often used for hoagie sandwich runs that didn't require the unhitching of a trailer.

Today there would be no foot-long sandwich run.

He started the engine and the moment his phone connected to the truck's Bluetooth he had it dial Ian.

"What's up?" his brother said by way of hello.

"Remember how you told me to watch out for anything going missing at Sky High?" Liam maneuvered the truck out of the parking area for the stock trailers and headed for the rodeo ground exit.

Ian was silent for a long minute, then said, "Yes."

"Amanda just called in a full-blown panic because when she arrived back home after competing in her first race that very nice new stallion of hers wasn't in the pasture she'd left him in."

"Whiskey Throttle? That's an expensive animal."

"For good reason." Liam turned on the main road and floored the gas. "With his blood lines and conformation, he'll bring in top stud fees." Either as a bucking horse or a barrel racer.

"Where is Amanda now? Is she alright?" The sound of Ian moving, opening a door and slamming it, came over the phone.

"She's shook. First the fire, now this. I told her to lock herself in the house with Honey."

"Good. Do you think she'll do it?"

Liam blew out a breath. "You know Amanda." But then he remembered the tremor in her voice. He increased the speed of his truck. "Actually, I think she will. With that due-on-demand promissory note appearing out of the blue, the cigarette butts at the edge of the fire… She's spooked."

"Okay. You get to her, and stay with her. I'll take care of the horse."

"What do you mean, take care of the horse? How? Do you know where he is?" Ian had somehow involved himself with cracking down on the selling of black market rodeo rough stock and bucking bull sperm, but was there more?

"No, I don't. Not presently. But I'll find out. And don't worry about how. I just need you to keep Amanda at Sky High."

"Should I call Caitlin?"

"No. She'll drop everything to try and fix this for Amanda. Let's see what we can do, first." The roar of an engine firing to life punctuated Ian's statement. It sounded a hell of a lot like one of their ATVs. Ian was likely heading over to the scene of the crime himself.

If there even had been a crime. Liam prayed there hadn't.

★

AMANDA HAD DONE as she'd been told and locked Honey and herself in the house.

And promptly went on the hunt for Uncle Red's bird rifle. As much as she hated invading his space, something she never had the need or desire to do because her uncle was an army-issue neat freak and wholly self-sufficient, she dove into his closet and peered under his bed. No rifle.

She sat back on her heels and gave herself a mental head-slap. Of course. He'd gone to Calgary. Prime ring-neck pheasant and grouse hunting in the wee hours before the start of the rodeo. She tried to remember if she'd seen his rifle on his truck's gun rack, but drew a blank.

So she'd have to settle for the next best thing. She hurried to the hall closet and pulled out her dad's old Louisville Slugger.

When in doubt, swing away.

Baseball bat in hand, Amanda took up a position at the front window. Just let anyone try to rustle any more of her horses or mess with her ranch in any way.

But a little, cowardly voice in her head started up the mantra, *Please hurry, Liam. Please hurry.*

When had she come to rely on Liam Neisson?

When she'd kissed him?

No. She'd kissed hot, bad boys before. Joe had been the baddest of the bad boys.

But never as she sat staring down at the airstrip. The last place she'd seen her parents alive. And by doing so, she'd let Liam in in a way she'd never let anyone in before. He understood the pain of loss. He'd suffered it in the worst way possible.

She stood at the window watching, waiting, slapping the bat against the palm of her hand while Honey stared up at her with two tennis balls in her mouth and her tail wagging—because, hey, balls and a bat equaled a hell of a game of fetch, right?

The roar of an engine over the fence ridge sent her heart racing. She stepped closer to the window and peered at the ridge.

The engine noise grew louder. An ATV?

A man wearing a cowboy hat on a four-wheeler rode up to the burned section of fence from the Wright Ranch side. The moment he stood and swung a leg over the seat Amanda knew who he was.

Ian.

Liam must have called his older brother. Who apparently had been at the Wright Ranch and much closer than Liam, who'd have to come from the High Desert Rodeo grounds. As much as she found herself wanting Liam with her to find her horse with his barn-burning bluster, Ian would do.

Amanda ran outside with Honey on her heels, but the second the golden retriever spotted Ian, she took off at her fastest run and reached Ian long before Amanda. Ian stepped through the fence and waited for Amanda with one hand on his hip and the other toying with one of Honey's silky ears.

Amanda was breathing hard by the time she reached them.

He gestured toward her. "Now there's a rustler deterrent."

She looked down and saw she still had the baseball bat gripped in her hand. Shrugging, she said, "I couldn't find Uncle Red's bird rifle."

"Probably for the best." He turned his attention back to the fence.

It was only then that she saw the gate she and Caitlin had used to visit each other most of their lives was tilted precariously, no longer resting against its latch or on all its hinges.

She knew the guys had struggled to close it last night, but had it been tilted that much? She honestly didn't know for sure.

Hope soared within her. Propping the baseball bat against the blackened wood of one of the fence posts, she asked, "Do you think Whiskey escaped through here?"

"Maybe. See all the fresh hoof prints here…" He pointed at the large prints made by a shod horse.

The day was quickly heating up and the mud created by the deluge of water they'd hit the fire with was rapidly hardening, but was still more than soft enough to be clearly imprinted by an eleven-hundred-pound horse. In places the mud was certainly soft enough to get all over her good boots.

"And over there." He drew her attention to the exact same prints on the other side of the teetering gate. "But I would expect a horse his size to flatten anything he wanted to get through, not squeeze his way past it."

Ian grabbed hold of the gate and tested its sturdiness. The whole gate promptly tipped all the way over, pulling free of its last hinge and falling to the mud with a plop. "And that leads me to think someone opened the gate, either led or drove Whiskey through, then propped it back up so your attention didn't go immediately here."

The hope that had surged through Amanda only seconds before dropped into the mud at her feet exactly how the gate had.

Someone had stolen her horse.

CHAPTER ELEVEN

I AN WALKED A few paces down the Wright Ranch side of the fence line, his attention fixed on the grass. With a jerk of his chin, he asked, "What does this look like to you?"

Amanda stepped around the gate lying flat in the mud and walked until she stood next to Ian. She followed his gaze down the fence line with hers. "Those are tire tracks." She glanced quickly up at Ian. "From the water tanker and Drew's truck?"

Ian shook his head. "Not that far down the fence line."

"Then those must be from the ATVs you guys ride to check the fence."

"The fainter ones inside the others are from ATVs." He pointed at a second, less noticeable set of tracks. "The four-wheelers have a narrower wheelbase. The fresher ones are from a larger vehicle. Like a truck."

"And a horse trailer?"

He nodded grimly. "And a horse trailer."

"Were those tracks there yesterday?"

He shifted his gaze to hers, his blue eyes troubled. "I'm not sure."

Amanda's stomach pitched. "Ian, do you think someone

drove up here, cased my ranch, and started the fire with the cigarettes, then came back and stole my best horse?"

He opened his mouth but the roar of a large pickup truck engine stopped him from answering.

Both turned toward her ranch and watched one of the black Wright Ranch dually trucks speed up her drive, gravel flying from its double rear wheels. It skidded to a stop in front of the ranch house and Liam burst from the truck, charging toward the front door.

Ian let loose a sharp, ear-piercing whistle that stopped Liam in his tracks. He turned and, spotting them, changed course but not speed.

Honey let out a happy bark and raced down the slope to greet him.

In the time it took Liam and Honey to reach them, Ian had lifted the gate out of the mud and returned it to its precarious tilt.

Breathing hard, Liam said, "What the hell, Amanda. I told you to stay inside."

"She came out armed." Ian pointed at the baseball bat propped against the fence.

Liam rolled his eyes skyward. "What am I going to do with you?" He said it like she was a toddler with a knife.

Indignation stiffened her spine. It was one thing for Ian to chastise her—he'd always acted the big brother. But not Liam. And her feelings for him had never been sisterly. Judging from the way he'd kissed her, his feelings, whatever they might be, were also far from brotherly.

Ian answered, "You're going to stay with her and make

sure no one makes off with anything else of hers, if that's indeed what happened."

"Of course I'm staying with her," Liam shot back. "That's without question. No way am I leaving her by herself with some thieving pyromaniac coming onto her ranch. Whoever he is will have to go through me next time." He met her gaze, his blue eyes hot.

Amanda's throat closed tightly. Who would protect her from Liam making off with her heart?

★

THE ADRENALINE THAT had fueled Liam from the moment he'd ended Amanda's call until he'd made it to Sky High Ranch and the fence line to join Ian and Amanda left Liam in a knee-weakening rush.

Normally, the void that remained after the adrenaline dump would have been filled by anger. But looking between Amanda and the baseball bat she'd considered protection almost made him want to laugh. Almost. Especially when she was still wearing her sparkly jeans, equally sparkly pink western shirt and, God help him, pink cowboy boots that would probably be sparkly too if not for the mud.

Liam pulled his cowboy hat from his head and ran a hand through his hair. Would this woman ever stop amazing him?

He met Amanda's gaze. He realized her dark eyes had a glint of topaz in the bright sunlight. Or was that her temper sparking in her beautiful eyes?

"Are you okay?" he asked.

She raised her arms with a jerk. "My horse is gone. No, I am not okay."

Definitely temper. Liam released his breath and a truckload of tension. Good. She was okay. She'd really scared him on the phone. He'd never heard Amanda Rodrigues sound so… *in need* before. The realization was sobering.

He settled his hat back on his head and looked at Ian and gestured to the gate. "So, what are you thinking?"

Ian pulled in a breath that expanded his chest. "Two things. Either the stallion shimmied his way through the gate, which looked like this when we got here." He pointed at the tilting gate and the roughly two-foot gap between it and the post it should have been fastened to. "Or someone opened the gate, led him out, and loaded him into something." Ian pointed to the flattened grass next to the fence line that looked like vehicle tracks "Then propped the gate like this to throw us off."

Liam went to the gate and tested its sturdiness. It fell over.

Ian said, "I knocked it off the last hinge that it was hanging by. Didn't take much."

Liam asked, "Why not just leave it open? It's not as if Amanda wasn't going to notice the horse was no longer in the pasture."

"Which is why I'm thinking two things. You know better than I do that horses are capable of some pretty wily things when they want something."

Remembering how Whiskey Throttle had run the length

of his paddock, seeming to chafe at its confines, Liam nodded at his brother. He then searched the ground on his family's ranch side of the fence for any other clues, like hoof prints heading for the hills.

Considering the gate in the mud as Honey sniffed at it, Ian said, "Amanda, your stud isn't by any chance a jumper, is he?"

"Not that I know of."

The idea of the big red stallion jumping the gate seemed unlikely.

Liam couldn't help but interject, "But according to Old Red he's one hell of a bucker."

Ian looked up, his sharp gaze bouncing between Amanda and Liam.

Exasperated, Liam said, "If I wanted her stallion—which I do, by the way—I would buy him from her by making her an offer she couldn't refuse."

Amanda scoffed. "You could try, Neisson."

Her spunk drove the exasperation right out of him. He gave her a slow, purposeful, head-to-toe appraisal. Damn, she was gorgeous. "You haven't heard my offer, yet."

He actually saw her swallow, and he felt it smack in the groin. *Now is not the time, Neisson.*

To Ian, she asked, "How would whoever he was get a truck and horse trailer on your property without someone noticing?"

Ian said, "This isn't the only gate in this fence line. And, ultimately, the Wright Ranch is a busy place."

Amanda shook her head. "I don't buy it. I tried to sneak

on and off this ranch often enough to know it's pretty impossible to do without someone noticing."

Liam chuckled. "That's because you're bad at it."

Ian gave her a *well, you are* look.

She huffed at both, then turned to look down on her ranch. "But why now? We've never had trouble with theft—" Amanda abruptly stopped speaking and looked at Ian.

It was clear to Liam she was thinking of the former Wright Ranch employee who had been stealing and then trying to sell prize rough stock and bull sperm. And had cost his family so much.

He shifted his gaze to Ian, also. Ian had known what the man had been up to when he'd been caught almost three months ago, but had refused to elaborate at the time. Liam wasn't about to let him off the hook now. "Do you think this is related to what Karl Fletcher was up to?"

Ian glanced at him, then shifted his gaze to the vehicle tracks in the grass. "It might. We know Fletch wasn't working alone."

"We?" Liam seized on the word. "Are you working with the rodeo association?"

"Among others." Ian crossed his arms over his chest.

Liam didn't know anyone as good at playing his cards close to his vest as his big brother.

"Are you saying my horse was stolen by some sort of crime syndicate?"

"Technically, yes. *If* he was stolen." Ian dropped his gaze back down to the ground as if the mud would offer up the answer.

Crime syndicate? Liam definitely wasn't leaving Amanda by herself.

Amanda buried her hands in her dark hair as if trying to keep her head from exploding. "If there is still a question about what happened to Whiskey, shouldn't we be searching for him over here?" She looked one way up the fence line and then the other. There was nothing but a sea of grass in either direction. "How big is this pasture? Is it even a pasture? You would think I'd know, but I don't."

Pulled toward her by her distress like a horse on a short lead, Liam went to Amanda.

Mindful to keep his grip gentle, he took hold of her upper biceps. "Think about it, Amanda. Whiskey was most likely taken. But we'll get him back."

Her gaze collided with his, her brown eyes swimming in unshed tears. "How, Liam?"

Ian said, "We're getting close to identifying the main players in this... gang, if you will."

Again with the we.

Ian went to his ATV, climbed aboard and started the four-wheeler. Over the roar of the engine, he said, "Just let me handle it, Amanda. Okay?"

An argument brewed in her eyes. Liam gave her arms a light squeeze, tempering it with a caress with his thumbs.

She surprised him by stepping toward him, wrapping her arms around his waist and burying her face against his chest. He instantly released his grip on her and wrapped his arms around her, holding her tight. She felt so good in his arms.

He dipped his head, smelling the faint grapefruit and

mint scent of her hair.

In a whisper, he said, "You'll get Whiskey Throttle back, Amanda. I promise."

He had no business promising her any such thing, but he couldn't help it. And he realized how sincerely he meant it.

And how much he never wanted to let her go.

★

EVERYWHERE AMANDA TURNED everything she'd worked for—her world—seemed to be falling apart. Except for here, in Liam's arms. Who would have thought?

She nuzzled against his hard chest, absorbing his strength, his heat, his scent. He'd used her uncle's toiletries, but on Liam they smelled so, so different. So appealing. So tempting.

If only she could unzip him and crawl right in and be forever safe from the world.

No. She wasn't that girl. She had a ranch to save and a top-tier stud to find. She could do this.

She leaned back and looked up at Liam, to tell him she was fine, that he didn't have to baby her.

He was looking over his shoulder at Ian, mouthing *I've got this. Go.*

Ian must have believed him, because she heard the rev of his engine as he turned the ATV around and drove away.

She gave Liam a light pinch. "The only thing you've got is a big head, Neisson."

He looked back down at her and saw her watching him.

He grinned.

Her heart thumped hard enough to knock over a barrel. She had to remind herself, *you are not that girl.*

She moved to step away from Liam, sliding her hands from his strong back to his lean hips. His arms resisted, keeping her close, but when she didn't melt back into him, he released her.

Honey immediately filled the space Amanda had created between them. Liam reached down and stroked the golden's silky head.

Feeling ragingly self-conscious, she asked, "Don't you have to get back to the rodeo and your broncs?"

He shook his head. "They're fine without me. Mitch and Jon can handle them."

Words she never thought she'd hear Liam say.

Needing to do something, anything, distracting, Amanda asked, "Now what?"

He pulled in a breath that expanded his broad chest beneath his western shirt. "Well…" He looked at the gate laying in the mud. "I'm thinking there is some fence work in our future."

"Shouldn't we at least try to look for Whiskey?"

"Amanda! How? Where? Do you think we can just drive around Pineville looking for a horse trailer with your stolen horse in it?"

The tears of frustration and fear and everything else she'd been feeling the past two days swelled again. She fought them with everything she had.

Her struggle must have shown because Liam reached out

and cupped her cheek with his hand. "Give Ian and whoever it is he's working with a chance."

She allowed herself a quick nuzzle into his hand before steeling herself and nodding in acquiescence.

He surprised her by leaning forward and dropping a quick kiss on her lips.

She swayed forward but he'd already straightened away.

"Atta girl. I don't suppose you and Red have some extra split-rail fencing stored in the giant old barn of yours?"

Relieved by his distraction and the knowledge that hard labor would keep her mind from her stomach-churning anxiety, she nodded. "This isn't some dog and pony operation over here at Sky High. Of course we have extra split-rail fencing."

Liam grinned, transforming his face from brooding gorgeous to just flat out, ridiculously gorgeous. He bent to give Honey, waiting patiently for more attention from him, a good scrub and pat. "Do you hear that, Honey girl? It seems you are not part of this operation."

"Oh, she is, but only because she doesn't consider herself a dog." Amanda turned and started back down the slope toward the stable, ranch house, and barn.

Liam's laughter followed her, lightening her mood further.

His long stride made it easy for him to catch up with her.

"I think I'd better change, first."

His gaze travel over her. "Yeah, probably a good idea. As cute as they are, those are not what I'd call fence building duds."

Pleasure flooded her. In all the years she'd known Liam, she couldn't remember him ever complimenting her on anything, let alone her outfit. What had changed?

He'd kissed her, that was what.

"You go change and I'll get the supplies together and load them—do you have a trailer for the ATVs?"

"Not a dog and pony operation, remember?"

"Right, forgive me." He touched his fingers to his hat in an acknowledging salute.

As they walked, Amanda told him where he'd find the ATV trailer, the necessary wood to replace the more badly damaged sections of the fence and gate, as well as the necessary tools and supplies. They left the pasture through the gate she had led Whiskey through that morning, only this time she left it standing open. When they passed the stable they split up, Amanda heading to the house and Liam to the barn.

Honey followed Liam, as any right-minded female would. Plus, the dog probably didn't want to risk being shut in the house again.

Amanda hurried into the house, stripping as she went. She grabbed her favorite work jeans, a fuchsia long-sleeve cotton shirt to protect her arms and her old brown boots. She put her hair in a low ponytail to keep it out of her face and settled her everyday brown cowboy hat on her head to protect her head and neck from the sun. She was tempted to step into the bathroom long enough to check her appearance but resisted. Liam had seen her at her absolute worst as well as her best.

She reminded herself she didn't care what he thought. It wasn't like she wanted to date him or anything. His being here was practical, for safety's sake. And she would be wise to guard her heart at all cost. She'd had enough hurt from loving to last her a lifetime.

Instead, she hurried into the kitchen and slapped together a couple of sandwiches made with the remainder of the deli meat Liam had snacked on and obviously liked the night before. He'd clearly been teasing when he'd claimed to have eaten it all. She seriously doubted he'd taken time to eat since this morning any more than she had. She placed the sandwiches and cold bottles of water from the fridge into a soft-sided cooler and hustled back outside.

Liam emerged from the barn with two five-gallon buckets filled with tools and supplies. He'd already hitched the flatbed two-wheel trailer to his ATV and loaded a large pile of fencing lumber onto it. The man worked fast.

She reached him as he set the buckets onto the trailer and eyed everything he'd gathered for the repair job. "You didn't leave me anything to do."

"There will be plenty for you to do up there." He hitched his chin toward the fence line as he secured the buckets and lumber to the trailer with bungie cords.

Fearing the only thing she'd manage to do at the fence line was ogle Liam as he worked in between scanning the horizon for Whiskey Throttle, Amanda headed toward her ATV.

"You don't need that one." He climbed aboard his four-wheeler and patted the seat behind him. "We can both ride on this one."

His expression seemed innocent enough, but there was heat in his blue eyes again that made some very specific parts of her very tingly.

When she continued to hesitate, he patted the seat again and beckoned her with a tilt of his head. "Come on."

Simultaneously thinking herself overly headstrong and a wimp, she gave in and, after placing the cooler in the trailer, climbed aboard his ATV behind him. The contour of the seat forced her flush against him and she was once again overwhelmed by the size, heat, and strength of him.

He started the engine. "Hang on," he said and released the clutch and turned the throttle.

The four-wheeler lurched forward and her need for self-preservation had her wrapping her arms around him and knocking her hat askew. She might not be *that girl*, but she sure did like being plastered against this guy.

Clearly mindful of the load they were towing, Liam drove slowly and carefully through the lower gate and up the slope, skirting the edges of the burned grass where they'd soaked the ground the most and the resulting mud was the thickest. He pulled alongside of the burned fence line, closest to the gate, because it would obviously require the most repair.

He shut off the ATV and when Amanda started to withdraw her hands from around his chest he stopped her by placing his calloused hands over hers.

Without turning, he said, "I really am going to do everything in my power to make everything all right for you,

Amanda."

His words sounded spoken from the heart and drew her against him once again. "I know, Liam. You're a good man."

He drew in a breath as if prepared to argue.

She stopped him. "You are. And you can't convince me otherwise. Now shut up and fix my fence."

He turned his head as much as he could toward her, a smile curling one corner of his mouth. "Yes, ma'am."

CHAPTER TWELVE

THE LATE SUMMER afternoon sun beat onto Liam's back as he lifted the repaired gate onto the new hinge Amanda had screwed into the fence post while he'd rebuilt parts of the gate. He tightened the screws holding the hinge to the fence post the rest of the way down while Amanda moved to the opposite side of the gate to realign the latch.

Sweat rolled down his back not only from the heat but the exertion.

He loved it.

Being productive, doing something, anything, to help Amanda, even in a small, way eased the frustration that had been twisting his insides over not being able to solve all her problems for her.

Amanda was working right alongside him. Her brunette hair, pulled into a ponytail at the nape of her neck, was darkened by sweat at her temples beneath her hat and her cheeks were dewy and flushed. In the past few years, he'd grown accustomed to only seeing her parade ready, lip gloss and sparkling eye shadow always in place. These last two days, witnessing her covered in soot, mud, and sweat, the reality of just how beautiful she really was hit him.

As did how well they worked together, mostly in companionable silence.

The fire hadn't actually damaged the fence as much as he'd feared. But the amount of water they'd sprayed on the area had loosened several of the fence posts and created enough nail-popping torque to damage parts of the fence and set the gate askew. Burned through or not, he'd still opted to replace much of the fence, though, to eliminate as much of the visual reminder of the last couple days for Amanda as possible. He knew how much such reminders could taint everything.

"Does fixing fences remind you of… you know… that day?" Amanda asked, seeming to read his mind.

So much for companionable silence.

He shifted to give her more of his back. "What day?" He knew exactly what day.

And he didn't want to talk about it.

"The day your mother was trampled by Blackjack." Her tone said she knew he knew, but was going to press him anyway.

She could try.

When he didn't respond she continued, "Weren't you about seventeen? Working on the corral fence? It had to have happened right in front of you."

He had been. And it did.

As if talking to herself, which she pretty much was as long as he remained silent, she said, "I would think working on fences would remind you of it."

Why had she decided to poke that particular wound

now? He turned the screw too hard and stripped it. He straightened in exasperation, and tossed the *remember when* game right back at her. "No more than you're reminded of your parents' plane crash every time you sit looking at that old airstrip." He gestured with the screwdriver at the ghost of the landing strip her father had cut into the earth.

When she said nothing in return, he glanced at her. She had turned to stare down at the landing strip and he realized it was just as much a scar she bore also.

Regret for what he'd said swamped him. He set the screwdriver atop the fence post and went to her. "Amanda—"

"When Uncle Red handed me the letter from the lawyer the first thing that popped into my head was that this was my chance. I could finally get rid of this." She gestured at the landing strip. "The due-on-demand note would be my excuse to just walk away." She leaned a shoulder against the fence post and heaved a sigh. "But I only thought about it for a second. Because I can't let this ranch go. This place is my parents' legacy, and I can't let them down. I want to make them proud. Losing this ranch is not what I want."

He was about to ask her what did she want, other than making her late parents proud, when she looked at him and asked, "Do you ever think about leaving the Wright Ranch? About going somewhere far from all the memories?"

"Of course. But that ranch is my home. It's where my life is. And my family. If I left… I can't make sure everyone I care about stays safe if I'm not there."

Her brown eyes were dark and turbulent in the shadow of her cowboy hat's brim. "You don't believe you could have saved her, do you?"

He hesitated.

"Oh, Liam." She reached for him, settling her hand on his chest.

She'd be able to feel his heart pounding from the painful memories, the guilt, but there was nothing he could do about it.

"You were seventeen—"

"And about as big as I am now." His age wasn't an excuse for failing his mother.

"Not even," she scoffed. "You were a seventeen-year-old kid and your grandfather's bull was huge and pissed off. You would have just been hurt, also, like Caitlin would have been if your mom hadn't pushed her out of the way."

The anger he used as his armor began to snap into place. "You don't know that." He turned away from her and went back to where he'd been working, snatching the screwdriver off the fence post. "Are you done with the latch? We need to finish up here and get the mares seen to if I'm going to have you at the engagement party on time."

"Yeah, I'm done." She gave the galvanized steel mechanism a good tug as proof. "But you don't need to stay. Go home and shower and change into something you haven't been wearing for two days straight. I'm more than capable of doing my chores and getting myself over to your house in time for the party."

"I know you are. That's not in question."

"Just because Ian—"

"Screw Ian. I'm not staying with you because Ian told me

to. I'm here because there is no way in hell I'm leaving you by yourself as long as there's even the slightest chance there's someone out there who is coming onto these ranches uninvited. Horse thief, arsonist, whatever. I'm not leaving you alone."

She smiled softly. "My angry guardian angel."

He huffed and started loading up the tools and supplies into the ATV trailer.

Amanda closed the gate, testing their handiwork by pushing and pulling. The latch and hinges held.

Liam pulled the combination padlock he'd found in the barn from one of the buckets. He held it up to her. "Fool me once… No one is getting this gate open who isn't supposed to."

"Including me? I don't know the combination to open that."

He turned it in his hand so she could see the backside of the lock. The special key needed to change the combination to the lock had been taped to the back of the lock.

She smiled. "Uncle Red at his finest."

"I always have liked him," Liam said and pulled the key off. He inserted the key into the bottom of the lock and turned it, then set the new combination. "I'm setting the combination to five, seven, ten."

Her smile widened as the significance of the numbers registered. "You remembered that Cait and I were born on the same day two months apart."

"Why wouldn't I remember? You two made such a big deal about it when you were little." He shrugged it off.

"Those numbers will be easy enough for our families to remember. Anyone else doesn't need to be coming through here."

"Now they'll just come right up the drive." Her tone was derisive.

"There is no reason to think anyone will be back."

She looked down at the stable, undoubtedly thinking of Rumbles, worth fifty thousand easily. Whiskey was worth double that.

"But that's why you're stuck with me."

She nodded, her expression pensive.

He threaded the padlock through the holes in the latch and snapped the lock closed, giving the combination wheel a spin.

He climbed aboard the ATV. "Come on."

She silently climbed aboard behind him and he noticed she didn't hold on to him as tightly as before as he drove them down to the stable gate. His disappointment was surprisingly profound. But what did he expect? He'd been a dick toward her.

Once through the lower gate, he stopped so she could climb off and close the gate behind them as soon as Honey was through. The golden retriever could easily slip through the fence, but Amanda waited for her regardless. The mares, either curious about the unusual activity or simply ready for their next meal, had all lined up at the fence of the back pasture and were watching intently.

He said, "I'll put this stuff"—he hitched a thumb at the trailer—"away then come help you with the horses."

"Okay."

Subdued Amanda worried him in a way spunky Amanda never did. He'd have to figure out a way to draw her back out.

While keeping his own emotions locked down tight.

★

After getting the other mares settled and fed in their stalls and paddocks, Amanda slowly poured a scoop of oats into Rumbles's feed bin, berating herself again for bringing up what had happened to Liam's mom. But everyone who'd known Liam before the incident knew he'd been profoundly affected by it.

He'd been an easygoing guy planning to take on the world as a bronc rider, excelling in both bareback and saddle bronc riding for his high school team as well as with the bucking horses on the Wright Ranch. After his mom was so horribly injured, he became angry. So angry. And stopped riding. At least he hadn't given up on his love for the bucking horses completely.

Warm hands closed over her shoulders, making her jump and sending the remaining rolled oats in the scoop flying.

"Oh, shit, I'm sorry," Liam said.

He slid his arms around her, grounding her in his embrace against his hard body and knocking her hat forward over her eyes.

The Liam she'd known three months ago would never have apologized for startling her.

She reached up and pulled her hat off. "No, I'm sorry."

"For what?"

"For bringing up… you know."

He dropped his chin onto her head. "And I'm sorry for throwing the airstrip back at you."

Her insides contracted as they always did at the mere mention of her dad's landing strip. Reputedly his pride and joy after the small airplane he'd built himself. Amanda closed her eyes and focused on Liam instead.

Her hair caught in his beard stubble and her breath caught in her throat. "It's been a long time since I've been in a *sorry off*."

He chuckled and she felt it from the top of her head where his warm breath tickled her scalp to the tip of her toes. "Same here. I'm not big on them. But I can't imagine you have much reason to apologize."

She rolled her eyes, but found herself relaxing back into him. "Do you not know me?"

He laughed outright. "Yeah, kinda." He seemed to sober, shifting his head until she could feel his lips on her hair. "I'd like to know you better, Amanda," he murmured.

She nearly dropped the grain scoop. A part of her desperately wanted him to know her, really know her. To know the gnawing loneliness that was growing like a cancer inside her, consuming her more quickly now that she was older and Red apparently felt free to finally make a life for himself away from her.

The other part of her, the part that she couldn't expose because those she truly cared for always left her, rebelled against opening herself up to anyone.

The one boy she'd let close in high school and for two years after had left her for a life away from Pineville. He hadn't even considered asking her to go with him.

Even Caitlin had left her when she'd gone away to school, only returning because her mother had finally started to lose her long fight with her injuries.

No, Amanda couldn't risk it.

Liam's mouth inched to her ear. The moist heat of his breath and the tickling gentleness of his lips loosened her knees and her resolve.

Maybe she could risk just a little.

She turned within his arms enough that she could meet his mouth with her own, kissing him deeply as if they'd never stopped when he'd first kissed her down by the airstrip.

He made a low noise in his throat and turned her completely, pressing her into him until her breasts were flattened against his chest and his groin was pressed against her belly. His arousal increased with every touch of their tongues.

Amanda dropped her hat so she could wrap her hands around the back of his neck.

Then his pants buzzed.

His phone, tucked into his front pocket, vibrated between them.

He ignored it, but Amanda couldn't and started to giggle. She tried to pull away from him but he held her close, kissing his way along her chin and down the side of her neck.

The thought of who might be calling him and why made

her push him away. "Liam, you should answer that."

"I'm busy." He gripped her by the bottom and lifted her enough that her hips were even with his.

She almost lost the ability to think. Almost. "What if it's Ian?"

"Don't care."

"What if he's found Whiskey Throttle?"

He froze for a moment, then slid her back down him. He released her and stepped away enough to fish the phone out of his pocket. He looked at the screen and huffed. "It's Drew."

He started to put the phone away in his *back* pocket, unanswered, his head dipping back toward her with the clear intent of resuming kissing her, but she stopped him with a hand on his chest. The feel of his thundering heart beneath her palm nearly made her reconsider stopping him, but now was not the time for her to take this particular risk.

If at all.

"With everything going on around here lately, you should answer that."

He relented with a sigh that sounded pulled from the soles of his boots. Keeping one hand in firm contact with the dip in her waist, he pushed the green button on the screen to connect the call.

"What, Drew?" His gaze settled on her lips as he listened to his second youngest brother.

They actually tingled in response.

Then he raised his gaze to the vaulted stable ceiling and released Amanda to push his hat up on his forehead. "Yes.

Tell her yes. I know. I *know*. We will be. I promise." His gaze dropped down to Amanda's, growing heated again. "No. I'll shower here. You're go-bag is still here. I'll change again when we get there."

Liam listened for a moment more. "Actually, that's a good idea. Tell Ian to send Mitch over if he's back from the rodeo grounds. If he's not, send Big Mike. Yeah. Tell her not to worry. And that she doesn't need to call, too. We'll be there in plenty of time." He ended the call without bothering to say goodbye.

Brothers.

"Let me guess. Caitlin is worried we won't make it over to the Wright Ranch before the start of the party."

"Correct." He slid his phone into the back pocket of his jeans.

"I'm surprised she didn't call herself."

"She would have, but she was sorting something out with the caterers."

Guilt washed over Amanda. "I should already be there helping her. I'm sure she's in a panic about having Bodie's family and yours all together in a confined space."

"I'm pretty sure the party is outside on the back patio where there's less furniture and artwork to break, so no worries there."

Amanda shook her head. Considering the person most likely to start a fight was standing right in front of her, maybe she should keep him here. Except for the look in his eyes when he mentioned showering…

No, they needed to get over to the Wright Ranch. She

was Caitlin's maid of honor, for heaven's sake. She had duties to fulfill and she was letting Caitlin down. But she hated leaving her horses and ranch unattended. Although, from what she'd heard, it seemed the Neisson boys had that covered also.

"Is one of your ranch hands going to stay here while we're at the party?"

"Yep. And will bring me a change of clothes." He looked down at himself, sweat-stained and streaked with soot and dirt.

She hadn't even noticed while plastered against him.

Glancing down at herself, she wasn't in any better shape. Heaven knew what she smelled like. "We need to get cleaned up."

He took hold of her waist again with one hand and used the other to push a lock of hair that had escaped her ponytail back over her ear. "We really should conserve water by showering together."

Amanda's mouth went dry at the image of them together in the shower, naked and soapy. She had to work at swallowing. "I'm not sure we would make it to the party on time."

He tugged her closer. "If at all."

"Exactly." She firmly stepped away. "Plus, Mitch or Big Mike will be showing up here at any time."

He heaved a sigh and bent to retrieve her cowboy hat and the grain scoop she'd unceremoniously dropped on the stable's concrete floor. "Fine." He swatted her hat against his leg to dislodge any bits of straw, hay, or dirt that might have clung to it. "Have it your way. But the next drought will be on your head." Liam punctuated his teasing pronouncement by planting her hat back on her head.

Amanda gaped at him. She honestly couldn't remember the last time she'd heard Liam tease anyone.

It was like seeing the sun after a long, terrible winter storm.

CHAPTER THIRTEEN

LIAM HADN'T SEEN Amanda since they'd returned to the Sky High ranch house right after Drew's phone call. She'd gone straight into the bathroom to shower, leaving him to wait for Big Mike, who'd arrived soon after with a change of clothes for Liam. Mitch had yet to return from the rodeo grounds, so Drew had sent Big Mike in Mitch's stead as Liam had requested. Big Mike, who wasn't actually all that big but had a knack for picking up very heavy things, also had a knack for noticing things. Perfect for keeping an eye on Sky High and Amanda's horses while they were gone.

Amanda had retreated into her bedroom straight from the shower, Liam assumed to finish getting ready for Bodie and Caitlin's engagement party, while he filled Big Mike in on what he needed to do. Which was pretty much just act as sentry while they were at the party.

Leaving Big Mike in the company of Honey to acquaint himself with the area around the house, stable, and old barn, Liam took his turn in the shower. The scent of Amanda's hair products, of Amanda, hung in the moist air in the bathroom. Yep, he would be taking a cold shower, and not because she'd used up the hot water but because he needed it after their latest kiss. The woman sure riled him up.

After he showered and shaved, he dressed in the pressed, dark-washed jeans, long-sleeve black button-down shirt, black dress cowboy boots, and the black cowboy hat Big Mike had brought with him. Liam's guess was that Ian or his dad had put together the outfit for him to wear to the engagement party. God only knew what sort of getup Drew would have put together. Odds were good a classic Nirvana T-shirt would have been involved somehow.

When Liam emerged from the bathroom, Amanda was still in her room. He went to her shut door and leaned close to listen. Nothing. He was tempted to knock on her bedroom door and ask if she was okay. The rational part of his brain said there was no way anything could have happened to her in the safety of her own bedroom. But then the guy part of his brain, admittedly most of it, went to all the things she might be doing in there—smoothing lotion on a sleek leg, pulling up snug jeans, snapping up the front of one of her sparkly tops over a lacy bra…

Liam turned on his boot heel and fled back down the short hall. They had somewhere they had to be. He planted himself on the couch he'd slept on the night before, which at the moment seemed a month ago, and resigned himself to wait.

Big Mike and his new best furry friend returned to the house, hesitating in the doorway at the sight of Liam sitting on the couch, his hat on his knee.

Liam beckoned him in. "Have a seat, Big Mike. We're waitin' on a woman."

Big Mike gave him a quick nod of complete understanding and came to sit next to him on the couch. Honey sat on the floor between them, as close to the couch as possible and positioned for optimal petting.

Liam resisted the urge to pull out his phone and check the time. Amanda would be ready when she was ready. He wouldn't be surprised if the phone rang with a call from his sister if Amanda took much longer.

She didn't.

The soft *snick* of her bedroom door opening and the click of heels on the hardwood floor drew his attention, so he and Big Mike, and the dog, were looking toward the hall when Amanda appeared in a silky, slinky, pale yellow sundress splashed all over with purplish pastel flowers. The hem swished about her calves, exposing not nearly enough of her pretty legs.

Liam's breath caught and held in his lungs. His blood raced. Damn.

She'd piled her mass of brunette curls on top of her head and wore low heeled, strappy, neutral-toned sandals on her feet. Her toe nails were painted a soft pink.

Big Mike blurted, "Wow."

Honey's tail thumped against the floor as if in approval.

Liam thought *shit, I'm in trouble.*

★

AMANDA FELT VERY much like a beauty pageant contestant standing in front of the judges while they inspected every inch of her. She'd made it onto enough rodeo royal courts to know what being judged felt like, but she'd always been wearing jeans, western-style shirts, and her boots. She felt downright naked in the silk spaghetti-strap sundress.

She desperately wanted to wipe her damp hands on her skirt, but she didn't. No way would she risk staining her new dress. She almost hadn't worn it, had actually taken it off and put it back on twice. Caitlin, who'd convinced her to buy the outfit when they'd been shopping for her maid of honor dress, had been adamant the dress and shoes looked good on Amanda and were perfect for the engagement party.

Faced with the wide-eyed, apparent shock of the two men on the couch, though, she wasn't so sure now.

"Maybe I should just go back and change into jeans—"

"No." Liam nearly shouted and bolted to his feet.

The force of his reaction sent Amanda back a step.

Big Mike simply shook his head adamantly. "Nope. Don't do it, Amanda. You look great."

She regained the step. "Thanks, Mike."

Liam moved toward her, his eyes glinting. A great mountain lion on the hunt. "He's right. You look great. Beautiful."

Heat pricked her cheeks and she dropped her gaze to her toes exposed in her sandals. At least she held her ground.

"Are you ready to go?"

"Yes."

He offered her his arm.

"Oh, wait. I need my shawl." She ran on her toes back to her room, irrationally unnerved by the sound of her heels on the hardwood floor. She snagged her dark lavender shawl off the end of her bed and hurried back out.

Liam was waiting by the door, his hat on his head.

The black hat and crisp black shirt made his blond hair and blue eyes pop. She had no words for what the dark-washed denim did for his lower half. He was so tall and lean and muscular. So tempting.

Liam smiled at her. Something she wasn't sure she'd ever get used to.

"Do you have everything?" he asked.

"Yes. No! My purse." Amanda spun and ran to her room once again, this time uncaring about the racket the strappy sandals made.

"You have a purse?" She heard Liam say.

Back in her room, she found the small clutch purse Caitlin had insisted Amanda also buy. She'd already filled it with her cell phone, lip gloss, and—just in case—breath mints. Judging from the way Liam had looked at her when he saw her in this dress, she'd need them.

The flush riding high in her cheeks spread, heating her throat and chest. And undeniable bubbles of excitement built in her stomach.

She was such an idiot. This wasn't a date, or anything.

Idiot or not, they needed to get to the Wright Ranch. She grabbed the clutch and hurried back out.

Big Mike watched her reemerge from the hall with unabashed interest. All he needed was a bucket of popcorn.

"Help yourself to whatever's in the fridge, Big Mike."

He grinned. "Thanks, Amanda."

"While keeping an eye out for anyone who doesn't belong or strange behavior from the horses," Liam interjected.

Big Mike sat straighter. "Of course, boss."

Amanda sent the ranch hand a smile of thanks.

He winked in return.

Amanda suppressed a snort. *Cowboys.*

Liam bent his arm again and offed her his elbow. "We should get going, Amanda. Kickoff is in ten and Caitlin is probably already starting to froth."

She surged toward him like she'd been hit with a cattle prod. "Oh, geez. I've been such a bad friend. And a worse maid of honor. I should have been there with her hours ago."

Liam opened the door for her and guided her through in front of him.

She held in a blissful sigh. *Cowboys.*

As he led her to his truck, he said, "It's not like you've just been sitting around with your finger in your ear, Amanda. You've been kinda busy with some pretty important stuff." He gestured with his free hand toward the burnt patch of field and the freshly reconstructed fence and gate.

She couldn't help letting her gaze drift to the stable and the empty paddock on the end. Her heart pinched in her chest and her throat closed tight. She hoped whoever had Whiskey Throttle was treating him well. If something happened to him…

"Hey." He gave her arm a little shake. "We'll get him back, Amanda. I trust Ian. You should, too."

She met his gaze. The strength and conviction there gave her a much needed jolt of determination.

He leaned down and dropped a quick, light kiss on her mouth that was almost as devastating as his deep passionate ones earlier in the stable.

"You *are* a good friend," he said. "I know for a fact Caitlin loves you. And you'll be a great maid of honor."

His gaze was so compelling, his conviction so strong, she found herself believing him.

He smiled at her in a way only a man who knew he just scored a point could. "Come on. Let's get you to a party."

He escorted her to the passenger side of the Wright Ranch dually truck he'd driven from the rodeo grounds. He opened the door and handed her up into the passenger seat. His touch lingered on her hand, her arm, her leg as he tucked her dress up out of the way of the door before he shut it.

Amanda allowed herself a full-body shudder of pleasure as he walked around to the driver's side. Once he'd climbed in, filling the cab of the truck with his presence, with all his manliness, she realized she could start redeeming herself as a maid of honor right here and now.

"So, Liam…"

He started the truck and cocked an eyebrow at her. "Yes, Amanda…"

"You're going to behave yourself tonight, right?"

He choked on a laugh. "With you looking like that? I make no promises," he said as he turned the truck and headed down the drive toward the county road.

He almost derailed her. Almost. "I'm referring to the Hadleys. Specifically your lone sister's soon-to-be husband. I know for a fact it would mean a lot to Caitlin if you got along with Bodie and his family at best. And not draw blood at worst."

Liam laughed out loud.

The sound filled up Amanda's chest with the warmest, best feeling. She wanted him to laugh more. A lot more. And she wanted to be the one to make him laugh.

A warning bell went off in her head. She was getting too attached, too emotionally involved. But this was Liam. How could she not?

"Sending someone to the hospital is the worst I could do. Drawing blood is nothing but another day on the ranch." He turned the truck onto the main road for the short drive to the entrance of his grandfather's much, much larger ranch.

Liam continued, "Don't worry, darlin'. Your days of breaking up fights between me and Bodie are over. Remember, I was there when the truth came out. You can reassure my sister that I will not destroy her future husband. Especially not after he saved her."

"More than once," Amanda reminded him to assure his good behavior.

He nodded, maybe a little begrudgingly. No doubt thinking he should have been the one to have saved his sister. Liam had a big dose of hero complex. But she got it. After watching his mother being trampled and being unable to do anything to save her, it stood to reason he'd feel the need to protect those he loved.

Whoa, girl. He didn't love her. He cared, she knew, but love? Her heart fluttered at the thought. A strange sort of fear and thrill converged inside her chest. Did she want him to love her? Did she want to love him?

Maybe. No. Yes. Ugh! The risk of loving and then having that love disappear made the fine hairs at her nape quiver with alarm.

Liam turned the truck onto the black-topped drive leading to the palatial Wright Ranch. At least compared to the rough spun Sky High Ranch, this place was huge.

The tall, elaborately scrolled, wrought-iron gate with the letter *W* worked into the design of the gate on one side and an *R* on the other had been left open, allowing unfettered access by those invited to the engagement party. Normally, the gate was kept closed, and only those who knew the code or had it programmed into their vehicles could enter. The rest had to be buzzed through.

There were already several cars and trucks Amanda didn't recognize parked in various places on the edges of the circular drive, with its life-size bronze statue of a rearing horse at its center, leading to the big house.

"Oh, no. We're late." Panic, intertwined with guilt, sent her heart racing and her blood pounding. She'd spent too much time agonizing over what to wear, how to do her hair. All with the hope of impressing the man next to her. What had she been thinking? Her focus should have been on being there for her best friend, not mooning over said best friend's brother.

"We are not late," Liam reassured her. "Those are probably just the caterers' cars."

"Parked out front?" she squeaked. "I don't think so. And

look, that truck says Hadley Cattle Company. Bodie's family is already here."

"If we were late, Caitlin would have called to make sure everything was okay."

Amanda wasn't convinced. "Not if she's too busy running around like a chicken with its head cut off. Just let me out here and I'll run in."

He shook his head adamantly. "Nope. I'm walking you in."

She couldn't contain her growl of frustration. "Why?" He was being so annoying.

The brim of his hat went up with his eyebrows. "Have you seen Bodie's brothers? Animals. Every one of them." He all but *tsked*.

She had seen the other Hadley men. And if by animal Liam meant hot and sexy, then *yeah*.

She looked at Liam anew. Was he being territorial? Over her?

A part of her whooped. Another part thought *uh-oh*.

But they had been kissing very, very passionately just a few hours ago, so she supposed it was only natural for him to be feeling a little possessive. It probably didn't mean a thing. And she definitely shouldn't be thinking about what they'd been doing before a party where she'd be surrounded by his family.

She willed him to hurry around the drive to the outlet that led to the vehicle and what they referred to as the "toy" garages on the side of the house. He parked the truck in front of one of the six tall bays of the huge vehicle garage.

The patio where the party was to be held was across the black-topped parking area and around the corner of the east wing of the house.

Amanda didn't wait for him to walk around the truck to open her door, instead jumping out on her own, her shawl trailing behind her. While she couldn't see the patio, she could hear music coming from the multitude of speakers surrounding the outdoor space. She knew it, they were late.

"Amanda, hold up." Liam hurried around the truck and grabbed the trailing end of her shawl to stop her. He stepped in front of her and reached around to drape the flimsy lavender material over her bare shoulders.

He did it with such care and gentleness she couldn't help but grow still and meet his gaze. The second she did she realized she was doomed. He was so handsome, so intent on her. Her heart broke into a full-speed gallop.

When his head dipped she lifted her chin and met his lips with hers. There was nothing quick or sweet about this kiss. And the fact they were kissing here, on his family's ranch, with his entire family just around the corner of the building sent her mind reeling.

She pulled away. "We have to get to the patio, Liam."

He said nothing, only raising a hand and skimming her cheekbone with the side of his thumb.

The sound of a car entering the circular drive seemed to shake him out of whatever it was he was thinking. He took her hand and slipped it into the crook of his arm again. They walked arm in arm to the path that lead around the corner of the house to the patio, a huge space delineated by concrete stamped with a light, grassy texture and tinted to match the arid natural landscape beyond the lush, well-irrigated lawn surrounding the main house.

Amanda gasped. They were indeed late. Or at least not arriving before some of the invited guests. A surprising fact considering there was currently a rodeo happening in the county.

Bodie, his brother Ben, and two of Bodie's wranglers, Danny and Cabe, were standing next to the stone-incased outdoor beer taps, drinking from full frosty mugs. Liam's brothers, Drew and Alec, home from school for the party, were leaning on the outdoor bar laughing with their cousins, J.D. and Jack. Liam's dad was talking with Bodie's parents next to a temporary buffet table staffed by the caterers. The men were dressed in varying degrees of formal western wear, meaning pressed, dark-washed jeans, crisp western-style button-down shirts, and their best cowboy hats. The older men were also wearing western-cut sport coats similar to the ones Thomas Wright usually wore. Bodie's mother was wearing an attractive cream pantsuit.

There was no sign of Caitlin or her grandfather.

Liam murmured, "It's fine, Amanda."

Bodie spotted them first. He approached them, offering Liam his hand. "Heard you two have had even more excitement today."

Liam accepted Bodie's hand and shook it. "We're handling it, Hadley."

Bodie's gaze shifted to Amanda. "Well, look at you. You're even prettier out of the saddle, Amanda." He leaned in and gave her a quick peck on the cheek.

"Thank you, Bodie." High praise from a former Rodeo Romeo.

Liam made a noise and Amanda shot him a glare. He was looking at Bodie as if mentally calculating the size of the hole he'd need to dig in the ground to stuff Bodie in.

Bodie grinned.

Amanda said, "I'm so sorry we're late. Is Caitlin inside?"

"You're not late. And she is, with Old Man Wright. Turns out getting him to mingle with a bunch of Hadleys is tougher than convincing him to accept just one."

Compassion overtook her worry about being late.

She put a hand on Bodie's arm. "Oh, Bodie, I'm sorry."

"It'll be fine. He'll come around. But Cait probably could use some reinforcements." Bodie looked pointedly at Liam. If Liam, of all the Neissons, spoke well of the Hadleys to his grandfather, then Thomas Wright just might reconsider his long-held grudge against the entire family.

Liam let out a very exasperated sounding breath, but said, "Okay, we'll help Caitlin." He settled a hand on the small of Amanda's back, his touch warm and possessive, and gently urged Amanda forward.

Bodie called after them, "That lip gloss is definitely your color, Liam. Good choice."

Amanda's gaze jumped to Liam in horror. He did indeed have some of her lip gloss on his mouth from kissing her. He wiped at his mouth with the back of his hand. When he saw the evidence on the skin of his hand, he looked at her. The glint in his eye wasn't very repentant and more than a little naughty. At her frown, he simply shrugged and urged her forward into the small crowd on the patio.

With nods and words of greeting to those they passed, they made their way to the French doors leading into the back of the house.

And collided with Garret Hadley, Bodie's oldest brother. Like Bodie, he was on the tall side with thick, dark hair. But whereas Bodie's eyes were the color of tempered steel, Garret's were darker, more like clouds before a storm.

"Whoa, there." Garrett grabbed hold of Amanda's arms as if to steady her even though Liam's hand was still on her back. Completely ignoring Liam, his gaze traveled over her. "Well, hello. Amanda Rodrigues, look at you all grown up and as gorgeous as a peach pie all ready to eat."

Amanda rolled her eyes. Clearly, Bodie had learned his Rodeo Romeo techniques close to home.

Liam surprised her by shoving between them, backing Garrett into the large breakfast room attached to the kitchen. "Step off, Hadley," he growled.

Garrett held up his hands, but definitely puffed up his chest. "What the hell, Neisson? Just complimenting a pretty lady."

"You can take your compliments and ram 'em up—"

Afraid of an imminent escalation, Amanda pushed her way between the two posturing men. "Easy, easy, boys. No one needs to ram anything." She sent Liam a glare. To Garrett, she said, "We're just on our way to find his sister, your future sister-in-law."

Clearly suitably chastised, Garret stepped to the side and

ushered them past him with a slight bow and a wave of his arm.

Amanda grabbed Liam's arm and tugged him by. When they reached the hall that separated the front, more formal living areas from the back of the house and connected the wings, she stopped.

She faced him and pointed a finger. "You promised me."

A smile played at the corners of his mouth. "I promised not to destroy Bodie."

"So help me, Liam—"

He silenced her with a kiss.

A deep, rumbling clearing of a throat separated them with a jolt.

Amanda turned to find Thomas Wright, Ian, and Caitlin standing in the hall, having just emerged from the den. Caitlin's mouth was hanging open while her grandfather was eyeing them speculatively.

Thomas said, "It's good to see you two were able to join us. I trust nothing else has gone missing or up in smoke at Sky High?"

Just my resistance to your grandson. And now she was going to have to answer for it.

CHAPTER FOURTEEN

"Nothing else stolen or up in smoke, sir." Liam tried to work up some contrition for having just been caught by his grandfather, brother, and sister, kissing her best friend in the hall, but couldn't quite manage it.

"No, sir," Amanda blurted, her face beet red.

Okay, he felt a little guilty over embarrassing her, but her blush mostly made him want to kiss her again.

Gripping her hands in front of her, Amanda said, "I'm so sorry we're late. We were... fixing the fence and the gate."

And making out like teenagers in the stable.

Mostly to Ian, Liam said, "I put a lock on the gate. The combination is the girls' birthday months and day."

Ian and their grandfather nodded approvingly. Caitlin was still gaping at him and Amanda, apparently slower to process what she'd just witnessed.

Liam continued, "I know it won't stop the serious types, but they'll have to work at least a little harder."

Grandfather said, "Good thinking, Liam."

His praise, which always had to be earned and wasn't easily given, made Liam stand a little taller.

Amanda asked, "Ian, have you found out anything about

Whiskey Throttle?"

"I haven't, Amanda. I'm sorry."

Her gaze dropped to the ground and without thinking Liam reached out to rub her back.

Grandfather said, "I'm sure that will change sooner rather than later. It's difficult to make off with an animal of that caliber nowadays." He moved past them. "Well, children, I do believe we have a patio full of guests we should attend to."

Ian followed their grandfather, but as he passed Amanda he said, "I promise I'll let you know the moment I hear anything."

"Thanks." She didn't sound encouraged.

Caitlin stepped up on Liam and poked him in the chest. "I want to talk to you later."

"Yes, ma'am." He didn't have to wonder what she had on her mind.

He was supposed to be keeping Amanda and her ranch safe, not getting busy with her. Nor losing his heart to her.

The thought set him back a step. *No. Not happening.* Or was it? He'd definitely have to think hard on the possibility when he wasn't within arm's reach of the woman who was making his pulse pound and twisting his emotions in knots.

Tossing him another sharp glare, Caitlin snagged Amanda's arm and towed her back toward the patio.

Liam started to follow in their wake when a knock on the house's large front door stopped him. Wondering who they'd invited who would feel the need to knock rather than simply walk in or go directly around the house to the patio,

Liam changed direction and went to answer the door.

He pulled it open and came face-to-face with a very beautiful woman with long, stick-straight black hair and large green eyes. She wore a plain black T-shirt and dark jeans.

She stuck out her hand. "Jessie Martin for Ian Neisson."

Liam shook her hand, her grip firm. "Nice to meet you, Jessie. I'm Liam Neisson."

She nodded as if she knew the name, but he was certain they'd never met. "Is Ian available? He wasn't answering his cell."

"I take it you're not here for the party?"

She looked behind her at the cars parked around the circular drive and Liam noticed for the first time a black truck with tinted windows and a white horse trailer hitched to it parked halfway around the circle. His senses sharpened instantly.

"Ah, no. I kind of figured my timing wasn't optimal. But Mr. Neisson—your brother—was adamant about being notified immediately when the horse was found…"

Liam's heart skipped a beat and he stepped past the woman to better see the trailer, but it was closed up tight. "Whiskey Throttle? You found Whiskey?"

"With the assistance of the local sheriff's department, yes."

As much as he wanted to run and get Amanda, he needed to be sure before he raised her hopes. "You're sure?"

"Yes. He was chipped and it was a simple matter of scanning him."

Elation zinged through him. "Please, come in. The horse's owner is here, also, so your timing is actually excellent."

"Thank you, but I'll wait by the trailer. If you could bring the owner out as well as Ian, I would appreciate it. Even though we have electronic confirmation, a positive ID by the owner would settle it."

"Of course. We'll be right out."

She raised a staying hand. "As discreetly as possible, please."

"I'll try."

"Thank you." She stepped back.

Feeling awkward about shutting the door on her, Liam left the front door open. He turned and ran for the back of the house. Only the caterers were in the kitchen so he continued out to the patio. Ian was talking with Garrett and Liam snapped his fingers at him to get his attention as he went by, his main objective being getting to Amanda as quickly as possible.

Not used to being snapped at, Ian frowned. But when Liam pointed toward the house and mouthed *out front, go*, Ian's expression cleared and he nodded.

Amanda was standing with Caitlin, a glass of beer in her hand, talking to Danny and Cabe.

He snagged her by the elbow. "You need to come with me."

Caitlin swatted at him. "Liam—"

"It's important, Caitlin." He leaned down and spoke close to Amanda's ear. "It's about Whiskey."

Amanda's eyes went wide. "What?"

He tugged on her again. "Just come with me."

She handed her beer to Caitlin and did as he asked. He slid his hand down to hers to lead her to the house. He didn't care if he was getting looks for holding hands with her.

Ian was already outside when they reached the open front door, talking with the Jessie Martin woman as they walked toward the horse trailer and black truck.

When Amanda saw the horse trailer in the drive she pulled her hand from his and broke into a run, the skirt of her yellow sundress billowing behind her. The clatter of her low heels on the walkway drew Ian and Jessie's attention. They stopped to wait for her but she ran right past them, straight for the trailer. Her hands fumbling, she unlatched and threw open the top half of the rear gate so she could peer inside.

Liam was pretty sure her squeal of delight was a positive identification.

He reached Ian and Jessie. He held out his hand to her. "Thank you. Seriously, thank you."

She shook his hand. "Just doing my job."

"Which is?"

Ian said, "Liam, this is Special Agent Jessie Martin, FBI."

Liam pulled his chin back. "FBI?"

She gave a quick nod, but didn't elaborate.

Liam looked to his brother, who supplied, "Interstate transportation of stolen cattle falls under the jurisdiction of the bureau."

At his raised brows, Agent Martin added, "The theft of your neighbor's stallion is related to a case we are currently investigating."

Liam looked to his brother again, but Ian gave away nothing.

Amanda ran up to them. "You found him! How did you find him?"

Ian went through the introductions again. "Amanda, this is Agent Jessie Martin—"

"Agent?" Amanda interrupted as she shook the agent's offered hand.

Liam said, "FBI."

Amanda blinked. "Wha—"

Obviously recognizing the circular nature of the conversation, Agent Martin held up a hand and explained, "We've had a number of individuals under surveillance relating to substantial thefts of cattle and rodeo rough stock in the ION territory—"

"ION?" Amanda interrupted again.

Ian said, "Idaho, Oregon, and Nevada."

Amanda's mouth formed a pretty little *o*.

The agent continued, "When one of those individuals appeared with a stallion of obvious quality in his possession, one matching the description of the horse Ian had alerted us as having been stolen, it was a simple solve."

"Did you catch the man who took Whiskey?" Amanda asked.

"We did. He is currently in custody. Our hope is that he will offer up the individuals heading this theft ring, but so far, he hasn't cooperated."

Liam asked, "Is he a smoker?"

Agent Martin nodded. "He is. And, yes, arson will be amongst the charges he will face."

Amanda grabbed hold of Liam's arm and bounced up and down. "They got him."

Liam covered Amanda's hands with his, incredibly happy for her but wondering what his brother had become involved with. And how.

"I hate to interrupt the party, but I'm sure that big fella"—she gestured to the trailer—"would appreciate being returned to his own stall."

Amanda looked to the open front door of the big house, her need to be present for Caitlin clear.

Ian stepped toward her, laying a hand on her shoulder, and said, "I'll explain everything to Caitlin."

"With discretion, please," Agent Martin repeated. "We can't afford to alert the other individuals involved in these thefts to our presence here."

Ian nodded. "Of course." To Amanda, he said, "Go. Take care of your horse."

Telling himself he wanted to make sure the horse was undamaged for her, Liam said, "I'll drive you back."

Agent Martin said, "We'll follow you."

Her use of *we* had Liam glancing back at the blacked-out windows of the truck she'd arrived in. He looked questioningly to Ian, who simply nodded toward the vehicle garage where Amanda was already heading for. Clearly, his curiosity would have to wait to be satisfied.

He thanked the agent again and hustled after Amanda.

She was already seated in his truck when he reached it, and, as soon as he climbed behind the wheel, she leaned toward him, wrapped her arms around, and kissed him hard.

The kiss was a manifestation of her joy from having her horse returned to her, but he couldn't deny the flip his heart performed in his chest. Or his need to deepen the contact.

But she pulled away. "Go, go, go! Who knows what Whiskey has gone through. I want to get him home."

He couldn't agree more, but the thought of no longer having an excuse to stick close to her wrapped his guts up in knots.

★

AMANDA SAT TWISTED in the passenger seat of Liam's truck, never once taking her eyes from the pickup truck pulling the trailer containing her precious horse for the entirety of the short trip to her ranch. She told herself the tingle and lightness engulfing her body was a result of the joy of having Whiskey back.

Not from kissing Liam, again, or the way he looked at her. Covered in mud and soot or gussied up, the hot, sexual intensity in his deep blue eyes never changed.

And she had no choice but admit how much she liked it. Liked it a lot.

Her gaze strayed to the man in question, so handsome and compelling, as he parked his truck in front of the house next to Big Mike's. The truck pulling her horse parked near the stable. He turned and his gaze collided with hers. There was that look again, but less predatory this time. More caring.

Her heart shuddered.

"You okay?" he asked. Definitely more caring.

Her throat closed up on her and she could only nod.

"Why don't you go in and change so you don't ruin your pretty dress and shoes. Big Mike and I will get Whiskey settled." He pointed toward the stable.

She looked where he pointed and saw Big Mike emerging from the stable door, Honey at his heel. He'd actually stayed in the stable to watch over her horses. She thought she might cry.

"It's okay, Amanda." He touched her lightly with his fingertips on the back of her exposed neck, drawing her gaze. "We've got this."

She swallowed hard and forced out, "Not on your life."

He grinned. "Figured you say that."

They both climbed from his truck as Agent Martin, who'd emerged from the passenger side of the truck Amanda now realized was an unmarked sheriff's vehicle, unlatched the top and bottom halves of the rear gate. With Big Mike's help she swung both sides open. Whiskey nickered loudly and the mares, closed up in their stalls, called back to him.

Big Mike looked inside the trailer and shot a fist pump into the air.

He glanced back at Liam and Amanda. "You found him!"

Amanda pointed to Agent Martin. "She found him."

Big Mike stuck out a paw and the agent gamely accepted his handshake.

When Amanda reached the back of the trailer, fully intending to step inside heels and all, Agent Martin stopped her.

"I have some paperwork I need you to sign, Miss Rodrigues, verifying this is the horse in question and that you took possession of him." She withdrew a folded piece of paper from her back pocket and unclipped a pen from the neckline of her black T-shirt.

Amanda hesitated. As much as she wanted to make everything official, she wanted to have her horse safe in his stall more.

Liam stepped past her. "I've got him." He didn't wait, but climbed into the trailer, murmuring softly to Whiskey as he eased to the horse's head and unclipped his lead.

Amanda and Agent Martin moved out of the way so Liam could back the big red stallion from the trailer. As if sensing he was back where he belonged, Whiskey cooperated nicely, though he kept up a steady conversation with the ladies in the barn. With Liam on one side and Big Mike on the other holding onto to Whiskey's halter, they walked the stallion into the stable.

Taking the paper and pen from the FBI agent, Amanda signed where she indicated. "I can't thank you enough. That horse represents my future."

"Then your future is bright, Miss Rodrigues." She accepted the paper and pen back from Amanda. From her other back pocket she produced a business card and held it out. "Here's my contact information. If you have any questions at all, feel free to call me."

Amanda took the card, but prayed she wouldn't need it. Despite the gravel working its way into her sandals, Amanda helped Agent Martin close up the back of the trailer. "Thank you again," she told her.

"Not a problem. Take care." The agent went back to the passenger side of the truck as the engine roared to life.

Amanda hurried into the stable and to Whiskey's stall on the opposite end. Both Liam and Big Mike were in the stall with the horse, running their hands all over him as he happily munched on a fresh leaf of hay. Honey sat outside the stall, her feathered tail sweeping the floor and her tongue lolling out of her mouth as she panted up at Amanda.

"Is he okay?"

Liam straightened and patted Whiskey on the neck. "He looks good. I don't see any sign of trauma."

She leaned her head against the side of the stall door as relief washed over her. "Thank goodness."

"You can head back to the ranch now, Big Mike. Thank you for doing this." Liam patted the other man on the back.

"No worries, boss."

Amanda moved to the side so they could leave the stall.

To Amanda, Big Mike said, "I'm glad you got your horse back. You have some really fine animals."

"Thanks, Big Mike. For everything."

He tugged at his hat and left.

Liam washed his hands in the utility sink then returned to stand next to her as she watched Whiskey eat.

Very aware of the man next to her, Amanda said, "Of all the problems I knew I'd have with this stallion, him being stolen by interstate rustlers wasn't one of them."

His hand settled on the small of her back and she could feel the heat of his fingers through the thin fabric of her dress. "Can't say I saw that coming, either."

His touch drifted upward along her spine, raising goose bumps on her skin.

"There are a lot of things I didn't see coming this week." He shifted his weight toward her. "Oh yeah?" His fingers reached the top of her dress, his touch featherlight on her skin.

She'd meant to bring up the letter from the promissory noteholder's lawyer, but she also meant what was happening between the two of them. What she wanted to happen.

"Yeah," was all she could manage.

Liam's fingers dipped beneath the fabric, caressing her in the most erotic way until she swayed toward him. As if she'd signaled him, he brought his hand up to the back of her neck and with his other hand took hold of her chin. Turning her face toward him he kissed her deeply, his tongue seeking and finding hers.

Amanda moaned, slid her hands up his broad shoulders to the back of his neck, and turned the rest of her body toward him, wanting as much contact with Liam as she could get.

He obliged her, pressing her back against the stall door. He was so hot and hard, everywhere, and every place he touched her, every time he touched her, she went up in flames.

She arched into him and the hand cupping her jaw slipped down her neck, skimmed her breast, lingered, then down to her waist, her hip. Then he was drawing the hem of her sundress up until he had access to her bare thigh. His fingers were like hot brands setting her on fire as he explored his way to the edge of her panties, dipping beneath them the same way as his other hand had the neckline of her dress.

She moaned again and he caught the back of her leg and lifted her knee to his hip, anchoring her weight, her heat, on his thigh.

Amanda pulled away from his kiss with a gasp and tilted her head back, overwhelmed by the storm of sensations he was creating. He used the opportunity to kiss his way down her neck and, after lifting her higher on his thigh, to her breast.

She wanted nothing more than for Liam to lower the top of her dress down and—

He pulled her hair where it was gathered atop her head.

Wait. He had one hand beneath her knee and she could feel the other splayed between her shoulder blades. How—

Her hair was tugged again, only this time the pull was accompanied by a huff of warm air.

"Ack!" Amanda wrapped both arms tightly around Liam's neck, pulling herself forward.

Liam straightened, bringing her with him, his confusion plain on his face.

"Whiskey's eating my hair!" She turned to look behind her, and sure enough, the stallion was standing at the stall door with his head over the curved bars that adorned the top of the wooden door.

Liam exploded in laughter, but released her leg to check for damage to her scalp. Undoubtedly coming away with a handful of horse spit, he turned them away from the stall and out of Whiskey's reach.

His gaze caught hers and his eyes were deep blue with passion. "How about we take this into the house?"

"Specifically my bedroom?"

"Specifically your bedroom."

Amanda smiled. "Yes, let's." She wanted this and would face whatever consequence that came from giving in to this need later.

CHAPTER FIFTEEN

ON THE VERGE of combusting from the passion Amanda had ignited in him, Liam wanted—no, needed—to get her into bed as fast as he could. Whether he should was a whole, separate issue.

He shoved aside his doubts.

Amanda still had her arms wrapped around his neck after pulling herself out of Whiskey's nibbling reach, but he nevertheless asked, "You hanging on?"

"Why?"

In answer, he slipped his hands beneath her bottom and hoisted her up, sliding his hand beneath her thighs to encourage her to straddle him. His head nearly exploded when his palms contacted her bare thighs beneath her dress.

She squawked, but being the excellent horsewoman she was, she wrapped her legs around his hips and gripped tightly.

"Wait, your hat." She tried to look around for the hat she'd knocked off his head. "Oh, geez, Honey has it."

He turned and found the dog holding his black dress hat by the brim in her mouth, her tail wagging madly. "Of course she does, she's a retriever."

"She'll ruin it."

"I have plenty of hats. Bring it in the house, Honey," he told the dog. He had a sneaking suspicion the hat was about to become his favorite hat, the dog slobber a reminder of having Amanda in his arms.

As if she understood, the golden retriever trotted ahead of him out of the stable. He followed the dog, making a mental note to come back out at some point and close the stable doors.

Amanda said, "Wait, I need to shut the doors." Clearly they were both feeling a little paranoid despite the horse thief having been caught. Agent Martin had said the man wasn't working alone.

Liam didn't want Amanda distracted with worry over her horses, so he stopped. As if a closed stable door would stop anyone truly intent on theft.

"You're going to have to put me down."

He kissed the side of her neck as he backtracked to the doors. "Not on your life." He let go of her with one hand—she squawked again and tightened her grip on him—and grabbed a door, sliding it into place. He repeated the process with the other door. The heat from where she pressed into his belly nearly undid him.

He regained his hold on her with both hands and leaned back to look into her beautiful face. "Better?"

She smiled and dropped a kiss on his mouth. "Yes. Thank you. Now take me to bed, cowboy." Her voice had deepened and grown husky, turning him on as much as her words.

He had never been happier to give a woman what she'd asked for.

He carried her to the ranch house as quickly as he dared, stealing kisses as he went. The dog, his hat still in her mouth, was waiting at the door. Luckily, Big Mike hadn't locked the front door so Liam was able to get it open quickly, letting Honey through first, and kicked it shut behind him.

"You can put me down, now," she said, nibbling on his ear.

Shudders of pleasure raced through him. "Not on your life," he repeated.

She actually giggled, her breath hot on his ear. Amanda was a lot of things—headstrong, willful, wildly independent—but a giggler she was not. The sound was intoxicating.

As he carried her down the short hall, he was seized with the need to discover if she was a screamer, too. While he seriously doubted it, she was far too in command of herself, he had a need to see if he could make her scream in pleasure.

He toed the door to her bedroom open, and once through, pushed it closed behind them. The dog would have to be content on her bed by the fireplace. She could turn his hat into a chew toy for all he cared, as long as she didn't interrupt them.

He laid Amanda atop her bed, covered in a rose-colored comforter that was surprisingly demure for a woman who favored sparkly jeans and satiny pink shirts with fringe. But he realized she wore those getups because she was more often than not on the royal court at the rodeos he primarily saw her at these days. The Amanda he knew now was far more practical.

But she certainly looked awfully pretty today.

Especially with her dark hair mussed from him—and the horse—her color high and one strap of her sundress slipped off her shoulder. "You are gorgeous, Amanda," he told her as he pulled her sandals off and toed his way out of his boots.

"So are you." She reached her hands up to him and he obliged her by settling on the bed next to her, one elbow propped beneath him.

He traced his fingers over her collarbone and the exposed skin of her chest the same way he'd explored her upper back and neck in the barn. Lured by the rise and fall of what lay beneath the silky fabric he slipped his fingers under the bodice of her dress. She wasn't wearing a bra and suddenly the need to touch more of her, to see more, to kiss all of her gripped him in a tight vice that threatened to rob him of the ability to breathe.

He pushed the narrow strap farther down her arm. "This needs to come off."

"I was thinking the same about your shirt." She tugged at the front of his shirt, pulling it from where it was tucked into his pants. "And your jeans." She hooked a bare foot behind his knee and pulled him onto her.

He accommodated her by rolling part of his weight on her, kissing her deeply. Which only made him want her naked more.

Breaking off the kiss, he rolled away from her. "I want this off." He pulled at the other strap.

She sat up. "It has to be unzipped." She turned enough

for him to access the tiny zipper at the back of her dress. It wasn't until he tried to get ahold of the little teardrop-shaped zipper pull that he realized his hands were shaking, and not just because he was about to come out of his skin with need for this woman.

Because she was brave, feisty, loyal Amanda, and he was falling in love with her. And that scared the hell out of him. But there was no way he could stop the raging storm brewing between them. He didn't want to. He embraced the storm and would worry about the aftermath, after.

★

How was it possible to be on fire yet shivering and covered with goose bumps at the same time? Her zipper undone, Amanda turned and looked back into the dark blue eyes of the man next to her and knew the answer.

It was possible because it was Liam on her bed, touching her, undressing her. As if every heated teenage dream she'd ever had about him was coming true. She was elated.

And terrified.

What was she doing?

His work-roughened fingers slid the straps of her sundress off her shoulders and down her arms, drawing the top of the dress down with them.

His hot gaze followed the progress of the silky fabric, lingering on her now bare breasts, and a fresh shudder of anticipation rippled through her.

Perhaps seeing her shiver, his gaze jumped back up to

hers, a question in his eyes.

Whatever he saw in her eyes sent him into action. He reared up and yanked the snaps of his black shirt open, exposing the smooth, muscled chest from her dreams. The shirt came off and went flying, then his jeans, boxers and socks followed and she had the absurd thought he would make a good fireman. But that wasn't right, because firemen get *dressed* quickly, not undressed—

Liam turned his attention back to her, pulling her sundress and panties from her and all thought left her head except for how sleek and beautiful and hard he looked.

And how wonderful he felt as he laid himself gently atop her and made love to her.

And how deeply she had fallen in love with him.

No matter how risky, how vulnerable the truth made her feel, she welcomed him into her heart.

★

LIAM AWOKE TO the sound of a dog barking and the smell of grapefruit and mint.

And the heavenly feel of Amanda in his arms, her naked bottom nuzzled up against the part of him that usually woke up first. Knowing exactly what he wanted to do with those parts, he pulled her closer.

A truck door slamming very close to the front of the house and Honey's barks yanked him out of his amorous state. Someone was here. He lifted his head enough to look at Amanda's face, but she was sound asleep, her breathing steady and deep. He wasn't surprised. They'd had a busy night.

Tenderness swelled in his chest. She'd given as well as taken. Eventually, they'd fallen asleep together, satisfied and complete. He never wanted to leave this bed. To leave her.

But someone was here.

Carefully untangling himself from the beautiful woman he fully intended to get busy with again as soon as possible, he eased himself from bed and peeked out the blinds.

Shit.

Caitlin, dressed in jeans, a white Henley, and cowboy boots with her long blond hair braided down her back, was heading up onto the porch. Amanda's shawl and small purse in her hand.

Liam gave himself a mental head slap. In the excitement of having Whiskey Throttle returned, and by an FBI agent, of all people, he hadn't noticed Amanda didn't have her things with her when they left the Wright Ranch the night before.

Moving as quietly as he could, Liam pulled on his jeans and his shirt. There was no point in pretending he wasn't there. Caitlin had parked next to his truck.

And based on her reaction to seeing him kiss Amanda in the hall at the Wright Ranch, she wasn't going to be happy. He wanted a chance to talk to her before Amanda had to face the ramifications of what they'd been up to last night. And early this morning.

A grin tugged at his mouth. Man, she was something.

Liam grabbed his socks and boots and left the bedroom

as quietly as he could, gently shutting the door behind him. The hardwood floor cold on his bare feet, he paused long enough to fasten his shirt closed. No need to further poke an already pissed bear.

He headed for the front door, thankful Honey's barks had turned to happy whimpers after she obviously realized who was trying the knob.

The door opened before he reached it.

Of course Caitlin knew where the spare key was hidden.

His sister froze at the sight of him. Her obvious surprise at finding him here, barefoot with bedhead, was short lived and the proverbial thunderclouds settled over her features.

For a split second he thought about lying to her, telling her that he'd spent the night on the couch, again, to make sure Whiskey was okay after his misadventures, but there was no point. She'd learn the truth about his feelings for Amanda eventually, anyhow.

"What the hell, Liam?"

He pointed to the open door and spoke quietly. "Let's take it outside. Amanda is still asleep."

Caitlin sputtered, but nonetheless turned on her boot heel and went back out the door. Honey bounded out with her. He'd have to find the dog's food and feed her, as well as the horses. The thought of doing so every morning filled his chest with a funny warmth.

The shawl and small purse still in her hand, Caitlin paced away down the porch, but the moment he latched the front door closed behind him she whirled to face him. "What the *hell*, Liam?" she repeated herself. "I thought I could trust you." She pointed a finger at him. "You told me I could trust you."

He buried his hands in the front pockets of his jeans, ready to wait for her to blow herself out.

"Of all the women you could use to get what you want, you go pick my best friend. My God, Liam, she grew up with us. Amanda is like a sister."

So not.

"She doesn't need this right now, not with that note on this ranch being called in and Whiskey not letting anyone ride him and then being stolen." She dropped her gaze to the shawl and purse. "You had to know she'd eventually sell him to you. You didn't have to sleep with her to get him."

Liam blinked at his sister. Were they talking about two different women? "Caitlin, it's true I wanted the horse. Still do, but—"

The storm roared back to life. "Enough, Liam. Just… shut it. Shut it." She stomped toward him, planting the shawl and purse against his chest where he had no choice but to grab them. "If you break Amanda's heart I will never speak to you again."

He watched her storm back to the truck she'd arrived in, a Hadley Cattle Company vehicle. Probably Bodie's.

There was no way he could promise not to break Amanda's heart. All he could promise was he'd do everything in his power not to. He had a huge learning curve to surmount because he'd spent too much of his life not giving a damn about anyone else's feelings. Until now. Now, she was everything to him.

And there was something he could do for her. There was one thing he knew he could break, and break well.

★

Amanda sat beneath the covers in the center of the bed with her knees drawn up to her chest. She'd heard every word Caitlin had said to Liam, having been woken by the click of her bedroom door shutting behind Liam after he left the room. Uncertainty and regret clawed through her.

Had he really slept with her to get to Whiskey Throttle? He had told her he'd make her an offer she couldn't refuse. It probably hadn't taken him long to figure out the one thing she'd never be able to refuse was a chance to be loved by him.

She was such a fool. Why had she thought she could count on love? Count on anyone ever staying? Her parents left, though she knew it wasn't by choice, but still. They were gone. Then her best friend left her behind. Her first love, Joe, left her and their small town behind for a different kind of life. Even Uncle Red was gone now more often than not. Why would she expect or believe that Liam would be an exception? He'd only wanted one thing from her. Whiskey Throttle. He'd as much as admitted it to Caitlin.

She didn't want to face Liam yet, so she lingered where she was as he returned into the house, set coffee to brew, then went back outside.

Maybe he intended to leave before she got up. But she didn't hear his truck start. So she took the opportunity to gather some clothes up, avoiding looking at the sex-mussed bed, and hurrying into the shower. She had to wash his scent, and her stupid hopes for what might have been, off her.

When she emerged from the bathroom, dressed in jeans and a plaid cotton shirt with her wet hair pulled into a ponytail, there was still no sign of Liam. His truck was visible through the front window, so he hadn't left while she showered.

She stepped outside onto the porch and her attention was immediately caught by activity in the corral.

What she saw knocked her back a step.

Liam was riding Whiskey Throttle around the corral. The big roan stallion would occasional kick out a hind leg or sidestep in rebellion, but for the most part, he appeared to accept not only the saddle but the rider on his back. In the length of a shower, Liam had broken Whiskey to the saddle.

The one thing Amanda had failed to do.

But she had tried to train the horse, not break him.

The thought of what Liam might have done to accomplish the feat, especially if he'd been angry at his sister, sent Amanda running to the corral.

"What did you do to him, Liam!"

He reined Whiskey to an easy stop, his grin wide. "Mornin', sunshine."

She climbed through the corral rails. "So help me, Liam, if you hurt my horse—"

"I did no such thing."

He dismounted in one fluid motion, and it occurred to

Amanda she couldn't remember the last time she'd seen Liam on a horse. He was always around his broncs, caring for them, but she never saw him riding. Even a saddle horse, which the Wright Ranch had at least a dozen of. He was always on an ATV around the ranch. Grudgingly, she admitted he looked good on her horse.

He led a very placid looking Whiskey toward her. "It seems he just needed a heavy seat. Some horses are like that. They think they can toss off any light-weighted rider. And they can, so they do. Like a pesky fly." He patted Whiskey on the neck. "Turns out he's a man's horse, is all. A big man." He grinned and she could swear he puffed out his chest.

"Are you saying you just saddled him, mounted, and Bob's your uncle, he let you ride him?"

"No, I'm not saying we didn't disagree a little." He turned and showed her his backside, filthy with dirt. Clearly he'd been thrown.

"Are you okay?" she asked, concern arcing through her despite her ire.

"I'm fine. And so is he. I didn't punish him or wear him out. I just climbed back on. He got the message that's how things were going to be. He's smart." Liam stroked the stallion's neck.

She threw up her hands. "Which means I'm still left with a horse I can't barrel race. Was this your plan? Break him to get him away from me?"

"What? No. I'm not saying he can't eventually be trained to be a barrel racer. In time, when he's used to being ridden, it might not matter who rides him."

"Might?" *Might* solved nothing for her.

"He'll still be an excellent stud for you, Amanda. And you have all the advertisement for your barrel racer program right there." Liam pointed at Rumbles, who he'd turned out into her paddock where she stood watching them, her ears twitching.

He was right. The only time Rumbles failed to post a top time was when Amanda screwed up.

She looked back at Liam, idly scratching Whiskey under the chin. "So you did this to fix things with your sister?"

"Heard that, did you?"

Her throat closed tightly when he didn't immediately refute her.

He stepped toward her. "I did it for you, Amanda." He handed her the reins, turned, and walked away.

Her stomach dropped. "So, now you're just going to leave, right?" Her voice cracked and she hated herself for it, hated that she wanted something she should know by now she could never have.

Someone who stayed.

He paused in the act of stepping through the corral fence rails. "No. I'm going to go shower. I'm pretty sure I have dirt in my ear." He tugged on an earlobe. "If that's okay with you, that is."

She nodded and put a hand to her mouth, struggling to keep it together. He was staying? Her world tilted. What did that mean?

He pulled his leg back through the railing and came to

her. "I'm not leaving, Amanda." He took hold of her arms and bent to settle his forehead on hers. "I'll do whatever it takes to prove that to you, however long it takes." He started to kiss her but the sound of a car coming up the drive stopped him. "Now what?"

Both turned as a black SUV pulled up. Thomas Wright, himself, climbed out from behind the wheel.

Liam sighed. "Thanks, Caitlin," he grumbled. Then he smiled at Amanda and took her hand. "Might as well deal with everyone today. Sure wish I'd taken time for coffee, though."

Not at all certain what to expect, Amanda appreciated the strength she received from Liam's grip on her hand.

Impeccably dressed, as usual, in a western-cut blazer, slacks, and cowboy hat and boots, Thomas strolled toward them, his expression inscrutable beneath his hat. He held a file folder in one hand.

Amanda's heart began to pound.

Thomas gestured to Whiskey. "That sure is a fine-looking horse, Amanda. Liam, I trust you've made sure he's unharmed after his little adventure?"

"Yes, sir. Of course. He's no worse the wear."

"Good. He'll make an excellent stud for both your programs."

Amanda frowned in confusion. "Both?"

"Your barrel racer and your"—he pointed at Liam—"bronc programs. It makes sense to combine the two over here. This is an excellent horse property."

Amanda looked at Liam to see if he was as confused as she was. His attention was intent on his grandfather.

Thomas came up to the corral fence and tapped the file folder on it. "Now, about that matter you came to see me regarding," he said to Amanda. "There have been some developments. After learning the noteholder, one"—he flipped the file open and read from it—"Robert Greenwood, had in fact, passed away and it was, in fact, his heir, Samuel Greenwood, who was calling the note due. Motivated by a rather serious gambling problem and in need of quick cash. Which I was able to supply. So the note has been paid in full and Sky High Ranch is free and clear."

Amanda couldn't breathe. It had happened. She'd lost her parents' ranch.

Liam started to speak but Thomas stopped him with a raised finger. "Having seen the affection blossom between the two of you over the years, and in earnest these past few days, I have decided the deed to this ranch will make an excellent engagement present. Hopefully, your party will not involve a visit from the FBI." He all but grumbled the last part.

He handed the folder to Liam through the fence, who released her hand to take it.

Thomas turned and walked away. "Don't forget you also have broncs currently competing in a rodeo, Liam," he said by way of farewell.

Amanda's mouth was hanging open, but she couldn't help it. She watched Thomas get into his SUV and drive away before being able to say, "What just happened?"

Liam flipped through the papers in the folder. "He's giving us the ranch as a wedding present."

"But we haven't even dated," Amanda squeaked.

Though the idea of marriage, to Liam, sent her pulse skittering and hope swelling in her heart.

Liam closed the file. "But I have known you most of your life, Amanda Rodrigues, and I realized last night how much I love you. I've loved you since you stepped between Bodie and me for sure, but probably even before that." He glanced down at the file. "Look, if you doubt me in any way, I'll sign the ranch over to you this second. Hell, I'll do it regardless. But I really do think you and I will be happy here. Together."

He stunned her further by dropping to one knee right there in the corral and taking her hand. "Will you marry me?"

Amanda thought she might faint; her heart was pounding so hard. She opened her mouth, to say what, she wasn't sure. But at that moment Whiskey Throttle stepped forward and snagged Liam's hat from his head, adding horse slobber to the dog spit already crusted on his poor hat.

The bemused expression on his face made Amanda's heart nearly burst with love for him.

She dropped to her knees and took his face in her hands. "Yes, Liam. I will marry you. But not in that hat." Then she kissed him.

THE END

Want more? Check out Caitlin and Bodie's story in *The Bull Rider's Second Chance*!

Join Tule Publishing's newsletter for more great reads and weekly deals!

If you enjoyed *Wrangling the Cowboy's Heart,* you'll love the other book in….

THE RODEO ROMEOS SERIES

Book 1: *The Bull Rider's Second Chance*

Book 2: *Wrangling the Cowboy's Heart*

Available now at your favorite online retailer!

ABOUT THE AUTHOR

Having never met an unhappy ending she couldn't mentally "fix," Leah Vale believes writing romance novels is the perfect job for her. A Pacific Northwest native with a B.A. in Communications from the University of Washington, she lives in Central Oregon, with a huge golden retriever who thinks he's a lap dog. While having the chance to share her "happy endings from scratch" is a dream come true, dinner generally has to come premade from the store.

Thank you for reading

WRANGLING THE COWBOY'S HEART

If you enjoyed this book, you can find more from all our great authors at TulePublishing.com, or from your favorite online retailer.